Schism

Gateway Series

Book 4

Brian Dorsey

Chapter 1

Emily Martin peered into the dim light of the hospital room.

The small light above the bed created a soft, white hue around Marshal Tyler Stone as he sat next to the unconscious Mori Skye.

Stone's head rested on the bed as he held Mori's hand. Since Mori's injury in the battle for Alpha Humana, Stone had spent every free moment with either her or his son, Octavius.

Martin exhaled; what she was about to tell him may change that.

She eased the door open and stepped inside.

"Sir," she said softly.

Stone raised his head. "What is it?"

"They've found him, sir...Maxa."

Stone sat up straight. The name of the man that had betrayed the Akota attack on Alpha Humana, costing thousands of Akota and Humani lives, caused Stone's face to grow red with anger. "Where?"

"Intel has determined he's on Bravo 8. It looks like Astra Varus has given him a small province from which he's begun to expand his influence."

Stone gently removed his hands from Mori's and rose to his feet. "How many men?"

"He has the hundred or so of his followers he took when he deserted but others have joined him as he's taken control of several towns and villages on Bravo 8…and he appears to have at least a battalion of Humani regulars supporting him."

"Payment for his treason," grumbled Stone.

Martin could see the rage radiating from Stone's eyes.

"Yes," she replied. "But I think it's time we paid him what he's really got coming to him."

After a heavy sigh, Stone sank back into his seat in frustration.

"Sir?"

"Maxa isn't important enough for the Akota to send a force after him right now and I…" he looked toward Mori. "I can't leave her."

Martin sighed. She respected him for his dedication to Mori and at the same time hated how the Akota witch maintained such a hold on him. "But I can."

Stone's gaze shot back toward Martin. "Emily?"

"I don't need an invasion force…or Akota permission." She walked to Stone, now on his feet again. "I'll make him pay," she said, placing her hand on his shoulder. "Just say the word and I'll find him and whisper your name to him as he takes his last breath."

She stared into his eyes; they were full of anger and pain.

He glanced toward the unconscious Mori, her amputated leg still wrapped in a regeneration chamber. "Go."

***

"Damn it," cursed Martin as she scanned the massive Akota mess hall. Since there was no social distinction between Akota officers and enlisted, they all dined together. Although the egalitarian practice was one of the few aspects of Akota military she actually liked, Martin let out a groan as she looked through the sea of Akota for one Iroqua.

Finally she saw him.

Martin's heart beat strong as she walked up to Thay.

Thay glanced up toward Martin and returned to his meal as if she wasn't there.

This wasn't going to be fun. She inhaled, swallowing her pride. "Can I sit?"

Thay looked up again, his lip curled with curiosity. "I don't control where you sit...the Humani are the ones that control all the little details of a person's life."

"Fine," grumbled Martin as she sat. "I need to talk to you—"

"About what?" asked Thay, still chewing his food.

Martin inhaled and slowly exhaled again, looking up toward the ceiling. "I don't feel like playing this game...do you want to go with me on a mission?"

3

"What mission?"

"To kill the man that betrayed our plans for the attack on Alpha Humana."

Thay stopped eating and looked toward Martin. "What's the plan?"

"He's on Bravo 8. We'll do a high altitude drop, find his base, and kill him."

"Who's on the team?"

"You and me."

Thay turned back toward his meal, finished chewing his food, and took a drink. "And why me?"

"I need someone I can trust to hold their own in a fight."

Taking another bite, Thay nodded. "Sure."

"Great," replied Martin. "We leave in two days."

"Good."

***

Astra Varus stood over an empty crib as General Vispa spoke.

"We have received word that shipments of the first wave of infected slaves have arrived and cleared medical checks at the demarcation stations on the Xen border, ProConsul."

"How many so far?"

"Fifteen thousand with another forty scheduled for this standard year, ProConsul."

Astra's eyes were locked on the empty crib. Octavius would be walking soon. Then speaking his first words...probably in some savage Terillian language.

Her hands gripped the rails of the crib, turning white.

"ProConsul?"

"What is it, Vispa?"

"Do you want the remainder of the briefing now or should I—"

Astra wiped a tear from her cheek and turned to face Vispa. "Continue."

"Yes, ProConsul. Construction at Dolus has returned to schedule and training of our modified troops is at full capacity. The first brigade of troops is ready for field testing."

"And where will this occur?"

"Marus Minor."

"Have we not removed that upstart from power?"

"No, ProConsul," replied Vispa. "We decided to let Bara Grimes continue to consolidate his position for the purpose of testing our troops there."

Bara Grimes was a two-bit idealist who had organized a small rebellion of miners and farmers on a planet within the Humana system. Vispa had been right to choose Marus Minor. It was completely under cognizance of Alpha Humana and not in either Xen territory or the Neutral Quadrant. And allowing Grimes to expand his influence on the backwater planet would provide a good test of her new Dog Soldiers. "I see. And when will they deploy."

"Within the month, ProConsul."

"Very well—" Astra noticed a young officer step into the entrance and come to attention.

"One of your officers is standing by to interrupt us, General."

"Very sorry, ProConsul," replied Vispa. "It must be very important."

"It had better be. Go," she said, waving her hand. "See what he wants."

Astra watched as Vispa walked over to the young officer. The officer saluted and presented a data pad to Vispa. Reading the pad, Vispa glanced back toward Astra and motioned for the officer to leave. The officer quickly complied as Vispa walked toward Astra.

"What is so important as to interrupt the ProConsul, General?"

Vispa looked up from the data pad. "Commander Skye has located a remote Terillian communications station. She is headed for the station with plans to take it and search for any information related to her mission."

"And by mission, you mean finding my son and the traitors who have him?"

"Yes, ProConsul."

"Commander Skye has permission to carry out any actions she feels necessary to capture the traitors and return my son."

"Yes, ProConsul."

"Is that all, General?"

"Yes, ProConsul."

"Very well. Keep me updated on Commander Skye's progress."

"Of course, ProConsul."

Astra gave Vispa the look that told him it was time for him to leave.

As the general exited the room, Astra turned back toward the crib.

"Bring him back to me, Sierra," she whispered.

***

Martin zipped her combat vest over her high-altitude jump suit and shoved a pistol into the holster on her vest. She pulled another pistol from the weapons locker and slid it into place in the holster attached to her right hip. Next, she grabbed her sword and attached it to the fitting on her back next to her parachute rig.

She slowly ran her hand over the three assault rifles in the locker before grabbing the one on the left. She took the rifle in her hands and placed the butt to her shoulder, looking down the barrel. Shifting her grip, Martin placed a magazine in the weapon and depressed the charging pin before attaching the D-rings to the slings on her vest.

Grabbing a combat knife, she held it to her face.

The mission was to find and kill Maxa, but her thoughts drifted to Astra Varus. Her heart quickened as she envisioned the blade sinking into Astra's body. She closed her eyes as her thoughts drifted back to her father's last moments. "Someday," she said softly. "Someday." She shoved the knife into its place on her vest and closed the locker.

Martin made her way down the passageway. Pushing the thoughts of her father's death and her need to avenge him from her mind, she refocused herself on the mission.

A few meters from the door to the jump chamber, she met Thay.

"You ready?" she asked.

"Of course," he replied flatly.

Martin opened the door to the chamber and they both stepped inside.

"Any updates?" asked Thay.

"Maxa is still in the Northeast area of the primary land mass on the northern hemisphere of the planet, near the city Fa-gra. He has several thousand men but most are out expanding his territory."

"How many at the command facility?"

"Unchanged, probably less than a hundred or so...mostly his men from before."

"Same drop area then?"

"Yep," replied Martin as she slid the air mask over her face.

"Weather?"

"Shitty."

"Typical," replied Thay, his voiced muffled by his mask.

Martin closed the inner door and activated the intercom. "Orion, we're ready."

"Standby," came Orion's voice. "Entering the upper atmosphere."

"Just one last thing," said Martin, turning toward Thay.

"What?"

"I get to kill him."

The light flashed green and outer door opened. "See you on the ground," said Martin into the comms link in her mask as she turned and leapt into the boundary between space and Bravo 8's atmosphere.

***

Freezing rain stung Martin's face as she reclined in the rough, tangled brush.

Looking through the viewing magnifier, she watched armed men moving about the camp a kilometer away. Martin and Thay had spent the last three days on the side of the ridge overlooking Maxa's headquarters. Her bones rattled from the frigid air and freezing rain but she welcomed the cold, wet, and windy weather over the recycled air in the metallic coffin of the transport.

"Want some?" asked Thay, reaching Martin a pemmican stick.

Martin grabbed the stick and bit off a chunk. As she chewed, the mixture of animal fat, oats, and berries consumed her senses of taste and smell. She hated to admit it but it was a vast improvement on the Humani 'food' sticks issued for missions when she was in the Guard.

"So why doesn't Stone do this himself?" asked Thay.

"He needed to stay with her," grumbled Martin through a mouthful of the pemmican.

"She'll heal or not regardless of his presence," replied Thay. "But for him to truly get vengeance he would need to do it himself."

"That's what I'm for."

"But how will his need to avenge Maxa's treachery be appeased by you?"

"Stone's not like us..." She paused, realizing she'd acknowledged the similarity between her and Thay. "...he isn't concerned about revenge. He wants justice...and I can give him that."

"There is no difference. Revenge is justice. The wrong must be avenged to return the balance." Thay paused. "He will never find balance."

"I don't think he want's balance," replied Martin. "He wants Maxa taken out because of the threat he poses, not because of what he has done."

"And you?"

"His pride and treachery resulted in the death of brother soldiers...so he deserves to die."

"Now that makes sense."

"But Stone is...he is more..."

"He's a complicated man, your Marshal Stone."

"He is," said Martin. "And he isn't mine."

Thay laughed.

"What?"

"Never mind."

"No," said Martin, turning toward Thay. "Why is that funny?"

"I don't know if you two were ever lovers—"

"No," snapped Martin. "That's just...no."

"Anyway," continued Thay, "regardless of that, I've never seen a subordinate so emotionally tied to a superior...its very un-Iroqua...or even Terillian in general."

"Well I'm not a fucking Terillian."

"But why do you...what is the hold he has on you?"

Martin thought back to the day as a cadet when service selection was made. "He gave me a chance when others wouldn't. I wasn't initially chosen to be in the Guard because of my family status."

Thay sat up slightly. "But why? You're an excellent warrior."

"Thank you," said Martin, surprised he gave her the satisfaction of a compliment. "First Family members get the first shot at everything. Another cadet was initially selected because of his family status…but Stone made them take me."

"Then you owe him a debt."

"No. He did it because it was the right thing to do. I just need…needed to prove to him and everyone else that it was the right decision."

"I think you've proven yourself by now."

Martin laughed. "My legacy will be how I prove myself."

"Legacy to who? Neither the Akota nor Iroqua give a shit about your family history…and you're with us now."

"I'm with you so that someday I can take my planet back from the First Family assholes that rule it."

The rattle and rumble of machinery in the distance drew Martin's attention. Looking down the ridge to her right, a column of tracked and wheeled vehicles, laden with produce and raw materials, came into view as it rolled down a dirt road toward the command post.

"Right on time," said Thay.

"Yep," replied Martin, taking another bite of pemmican. "Three days in a row they head out at 1000 local and comeback a few hours later."

"They must be collecting supplies from nearby villages."

"Well, three times is a trend," said Martin. Over the last three days they'd watched convoys of vehicles leaving and entering the camp, observed guard turnovers, identified defensive positions, and planned their path to carry out their mission. "Do we need to observe anymore?"

"No," replied Thay. "Tomorrow?"

"Tomorrow."

The supply convoy would be their way in.

***

Martin crouched low as the column of trucks rolled past, the occasional rattle of metal or splash of mud punctuating the rumble of their engines. She focused on the final vehicle as it neared the marker of broken branches she'd placed near the road.

The truck reached the mark and Martin activated the detonator.

A small pop was immediately followed by the sound of a tire rupturing.

Martin shouldered her rifle and waited for the truck to come to a stop. Her rifle centered on the driver, she watched as he hopped onto the muddy road and inspected the tire.

"Shit," cursed the man.

"What is it?" asked the passenger as he joined the driver.

"Tire's shot," replied the driver, pulling a large piece of metal out of the muck. "Must have hit this."

Martin had set up the scenario well.

'Truck seven, this is truck one. What's your status?' came over the driver's radio.

"Flat tire," replied the driver.

'Do you need help?'

"No," sighed the driver. "We'll change it and catch up."

Kicking the wheel of the flat tire, the driver knelt down and looked up toward the passenger. "Grab the tools."

Martin drew her sword and tightened her body, ready to leap from her position.

Thay's hand on her shoulder stopped her.

"Let them change to the tire," he mouthed. "Unless you want to do it."

Martin nodded in agreement. No need for extra work.

In a few minutes, the job was done and the men began to store their tools.

"We're gonna be late for chow," huffed the passenger as he turned toward the back of the truck. "I just—"

Martin burst from the cover of the forest toward the truck.

The passenger grabbed the rifle strapped across his torso but he stumbled backwards, falling against the truck with Thay's tomahawk protruding from his chest.

The driver, startled by the sight of the passenger falling, was slow to react but swung his body toward the threat with a pistol in his hand.

An upward slash from Martin's sword separated the driver's hand from his arm. She pivoted and snapped her torso, laying open his chest with another stroke of her sword. As the man fell to his knees, she drove her sword through her opponent's neck. Letting out a grunt, she twisted the sword and yanked it from the man's body. As the driver fell to the ground, Martin looked up to see Thay standing over the passenger.

"Well that was easy enough," said Thay, wiping the blade of his tomahawk.

"Let's get enough of their clothes to pass for Maxa's men," said Martin, pulling at the driver's coat.

"Hopefully they won't notice the blood."

"We just need to get through the gate and we'll be good." Martin paused, looking up toward Thay. "Then the blood won't matter."

Chapter 2

The side-to-side motion of the wipers pushed the thick streams of rainwater away from the windshield as the command post came into sight. Glancing away from the road, Martin looked down to the rifle laying on the seat between her and Thay. "Ready?"

Thay responded with a smile.

"All right…let's do this," said Martin as the truck approached the security checkpoint.

Martin slid her right hand to the pistol in her lap as she let her foot slide off the accelerator, slowing the truck.

A guard near the gate quickly stepped into the rain from a covered shack and waved the truck forward.

"Alright then," said Martin out loud as the gate began to slide open.

"Guess he didn't want to get wet," added Thay.

"His laziness might've just saved his life," replied Martin as she began to increase the speed of the truck and passed through the gate.

Thay positioned his rifle in preparation to exit the truck. "Maybe…maybe not."

With the mental map of the camp solid in her head from three days of observation, Martin drove the truck through the camp to the back of a small utility building and stopped.

16

"This is you."

"Comms good?" Thay spoke into the link over his throat.

"Good," replied Martin, hearing Thay's voice in her earpiece. "Happy hunting."

Thay gave her a smile and jumped from the truck into the downpour.

With Thay off to plant diversionary explosives and cover their escape, Martin pulled the truck into the parking area behind the building they'd identified as Maxa's headquarters. Turning off the engine, Martin stepped out of the truck with a splash as her feet hit the small river of water flowing through the parking lot. Closing the door, she sensed someone behind her and turned to see a man wearing an officer's uniform.

"You can't park that here," barked the man. "This area's for officers only."

Martin's hand gripped her pistol underneath the raincoat. "I'm sorry...I was just—"

"You're a woman," said the man, his brow furrowed. "What unit are you with?" demanded the officer.

"I...uh...fuck it," grunted Martin as she crashed her boot into the man's knee, causing him to fall to his knees. As he fell, she grabbed the side of his head and slammed it against the truck. Pulling his torso away from the truck, Martin wrapped her arms around his neck and locked them in place. She grunted as she tightened her muscles around his neck.

In a few seconds, he was unconscious.

Martin scanned the area. There was nothing but the rain and windswept puddles of water. She examined the man's overcoat then glanced at the one she was wearing. Hers was muddy and still had remnants of blood despite the deluge.

Martin tossed her coat into the truck and pulled the raincoat off the man. Lifting him into her arms, she shoved the officer into the cab of the truck. Slamming the door, Martin turned into a wave of water as another truck splashed to a stop next to her.

"Shit," she cursed, turning away from the wall of water as it crashed against her coat.

The icy water soaked through her pants and down to her socks as she faced the truck.

The passenger door swung open and a stocky man leapt out, sending another splash of water against her legs. She glanced down toward her soaked pants and then slowly raised her head until she met the gaze of the man standing across from her. She stared quietly at him as the rain pelted her face. Looking past the man, she saw another soldier appear from the front of the truck.

"Faris," said a tall, wiry soldier as he sloshed through the puddles. "Get our cargo. General Maxa is—" He paused when he saw Martin. "And who is this?"

"I'm new," replied Martin. "Just transferred—"

"There's no women in Maxa's army," said the stocky soldier, his eyes tightening.

"I…I'm the general's new secretary." Martin wrapped her hand around the handle of her knife underneath her coat as she visualized how she would kill both of them.

"Secretary," laughed the stocky soldier. "Sure."

"Well," said the other soldier. "Must be good to be the king." He turned toward his companion. "Guess we should get the other one up there."

Martin watched as the men walked to the back of the covered truck and emerged with a young woman in tow.

"Another one for the collection," said the stocky soldier with a glance toward Martin as they passed.

The woman's face was twisted with anxiety and fear as the two soldiers led her past Martin and toward the rear entrance of the building. Releasing the grip on her knife and sliding her hand to her pistol, Martin followed them.

As they entered the building, the low roar of the rain disappeared and the cold bite of the wind was replaced with a warmth she hadn't felt in days.

"You're a lucky one. At least you don't have to stay in the stables," said the tall soldier.

"Stables?" asked Martin.

Both soldiers laughed.

Martin knew what they meant. She looked toward the woman; she knew too.

Without a word the four walked up a set of stairs, stopping near a set of double doors.

"Here ya go, sweetheart," said the stocky guard to the woman. "And I guess you'll be heading up to take some…dictation," he smiled as he looked toward Martin.

Ignoring the man, Martin glanced toward the young woman. Her eyes screamed for help—for someone to save her from what was to come.

The tall guard opened the doors. Inside, another guard stood in the middle of a large room with cages along the walls. Most of them contained women.

Martin's body tightened with anger but she couldn't react without giving herself away. With a sigh, she stepped around the soldiers to continue her search for Maxa.

"Say hello to the general for us," said the tall soldier as he shoved the woman into the room.

Martin continued to walk away, closing her eyes in an attempt to clear her mind of the woman's fate.

She heard the soldiers continue to talk.

"Sergeant said he gives his leftovers to his officers after he's done with them," said the stocky soldier as he closed the door behind them.

Martin stopped.

She paced in a circle in the passageway before facing the double doors. "Damn it," she grumbled as she let her overcoat fall to the floor.

Martin drew her sword as she crept toward the door. Maybe by saving the young woman she could make up for what had happened in another room on a cold, remote planet years before. She placed her hand on the handle but paused as the vision of the young Phelian girl from so long ago flashed into her consciousness. Her pulse quickened.

She turned the handle and burst into the room.

The stocky soldier, still holding the woman's arm, turned toward the door just as Martin drove her sword through his side. Feeling the hilt contact the soldier's ribs, she twisted her hips, jerked the sword from his body, and sliced through the other soldier's chest in one motion.

Martin shifted her weight to her back foot and then thrust forward, plunging her sword into the abdomen of the last guard. As he gasped, she withdrew the sword, cocked it above her head, and slashed downward, laying open the man's torso.

Martin turned toward the woman, who stumbled backwards, falling to the ground.

"Stop!" ordered Martin, seeing the woman brought in by the guards was about to scream. "Stop!" she said again, lowering her sword.

The woman complied but scooted away from Martin. She jerked when her back made contact with one of the cages. She saw a woman curled in the corner of the cage and let out a gasp before turning back toward Martin with wide, frightened eyes.

"I'm not going to hurt you," said Martin. "Just stay calm," she continued as she turned to shut the door.

"I need to get out of here," cried the woman as she pulled herself to her feet. "I have to go." She rushed for the exit.

"I know," said Martin as she stepped in front of the door. Martin placed her hand on the woman's shoulder. "But I need you to stay here for just a minute."

"Stay? I—"

"I'll help you get out of here. I promise. But I have to do something first and can't have you and the others running around alerting anyone…just please wait so I—"

"Emily?"

A familiar voice caused Martin to spin around to one of the cages. Her sword fell to the floor. "Aria?"

Despite the tangled hair and filth, Martin recognized the woman in a torn and tattered dress. The eyes were unmistakable. Martin forgot about the woman trying to escape as she realized she was looking at her cousin, Aria. "What—how did you get here? Are you okay?"

"How did you know I was here?" huffed Aria, tears flowing down her face. "I never thought—"

"I'm here for Maxa…I didn't know…what happened?"

"What happened?" repeated Aria, her pitch higher.

Martin had not seen Aria since the day the suicide bomber had killed so many on Alpha Humana. "How did you—?"

Aria's expression tightened. "You happened," she snapped, anger replacing relief.

"What?"

"What do you think would happen when you took the ProConsul's son?"

"I—" Martin paused. She hadn't thought about—. "Wait!" she ordered turning back to the captive woman as Martin saw her step toward the door. "Please."

The woman stopped and Martin turned back toward Aria. "She had my father killed and I—"

"Your father," grumbled Aria. "That alcoholic was already dead; he just didn't know it…but the rest of us…" Aria gripped the bars of her cell. "When you took the

23

ProConsul's son she focused all of her rage on the Martin family."

Martin involuntarily took a step backwards. She'd never really cared too much about most of her family but she hadn't thought about what Astra Varus would do to her kin in the name of vengeance. "I didn't—"

"Half the men just disappeared and the children were placed in rural orphanages."

"No," mouthed Martin. How could she have not realized what Astra Varus would do?

"Yes," growled Aria. "And then she…" Aria lowered her head momentarily. When she raised her head to meet Martin's gaze, her eyes were distant, reliving a pain that tore at her soul. "…she gave me to Maxa as a present for telling her about the attack."

"I—"

"When he had enough of me…he gave me to his officers for their…for their…" Aria fell silent.

"I'm sorry. I—"

"You've destroyed your entire family with your actions, Emily," continued Aria, her eyes still locked on her past horror. "Your treason has ended us…" Aria turned her gaze to Martin, the pain and anger burned at Martin's soul. "…I just wasn't lucky enough to die."

"I…I'll get you out of here."

"And where will I go?"

Martin stepped toward the cage. "I'll get you to safety, Aria. I—"

"Just do the one thing you're good at, Emily…"

"Aria? What do you—"

"Killing, my dear cousin," spat Aria. "Killing is what you are good at. So kill Maxa and…all of them."

Martin lowered her head, her heart aching. She couldn't take back all of the pain her actions had caused her family.

But she could avenge it.

She raised her head. "I will kill him," she said softly.

Martin took the keys from the dead guard and opened Aria's cell. "Let the others free and stay here until I come back. I promise—"

Martin saw the young woman moving toward the door again. "Wait please." She turned and rushed to the door, grabbing the woman's arm. "Please…just a few minutes."

"Emily…"

Martin turned toward Aria.

Aria stood next to her cell with one of the soldier's knives held to her neck.

"Aria? What are you doing?"

"There is no life for me anymore…nowhere to live where I can forget…I can't forget…" Aria closed her eyes and raised her head toward the ceiling.

"No, Aria…you can—"

"Kill Maxa," interrupted Aria. "And remember this when you're doing it."

"No!" shouted Martin as Aria pulled the blade across her throat.

Blood pumped from Aria's neck as she fell to the floor.

Martin rushed to her cousin. Taking Aria in her arms, she tried to apply pressure to the gash in her cousin's neck as blood sprayed over her face. "No. No. No," panted Martin as she reached for her medical kit. "Shit!" she cursed realizing she'd left it in the truck.

Tears flowed down Martin's face as she watched the life fade from Aria's eyes.

Lowering her cousin's body to the floor, she looked up toward the ceiling.

Martin exhaled heavily and rose to her feet, wiping the tears from her face. As she looked at her sleeves, Martin saw Aria's blood smeared into the fabric. She stared at the blood; blood that was both literally and figuratively on her hands.

Then a clarity struck her.

Martin picked up her sword and looked toward the woman. "Here," she said, tossing the keys to her. "Let the others free and get out of this building."

Her cousin was right. Martin was good at one thing…killing.

"Thay," she spoke into the comms link. "Change of plans—"

Martin leapt forward into a roll as another guard stepped into the room.

Before he could react, Martin knocked the rifle from the guard's hands and landed a straight kick into his sternum, knocking him against the wall. The guard reached for his pistol but Martin lunged forward.

The guard let out a guttural groan as Martin's sword sank into his stomach.

Martin pushed forward, driving the tip of her sword through the guard and into the wall behind him.

The man let out a cry but Martin's pressed her hand over his mouth, silencing him. She twisted the blade, watching his face contort with pain as the warm saliva from the man's muffled scream wet her hand.

Tears clouded Martin's vision as she leaned in close to the guard's face and activated her comms link. "—I'm going to kill all of them."

***

Martin crouched low as she crept down the stairway leading to the third floor of the building where she hoped to find Maxa. Her jaw clamped tight in anger as she fought to push the vision of Aria's vacant stare from her mind.

As she turned the corner to the stairway, Martin was met by two officers. Their eyes widened when they saw the blood-soaked Martin in front of them. "Stop!" shouted one of them as he attempted to draw his sidearm.

Martin rushed forward and leapt into the air, knocking both men through the double doors and into the vestibule for the stairway.

The officer to the right was pushing himself off the floor when Martin pivoted her body and drove her knee into his temple, driving his head against the wall. She turned toward the second man and grabbed his hand as he swung his pistol toward her.

Wrenching her opponent's hand backwards and extending the man's arm above his shoulder, Martin drove her knee upward, slamming it into her opponent's chin. As his head snapped backwards, she ripped the pistol from his hand and twisted her body to drive him to the ground. When the officer's body hit the floor, she drove her boot into his shoulder as she yanked hard on his arm. The ripping of ligaments echoed through the vestibule and her opponent let out a shriek of agony that was silenced when she raised her foot again and crashed it into the back of his head.

Turning back toward the first officer, Martin caught him just as he rose to his feet. He swung wildly at her but she deflected his attack, shoved him face-first against the wall, and landed two powerful blows to his kidneys.

As his body arched away from the blows, Martin grabbed his right arm and spun him away from the wall. Using the momentum she had created, she twisted his arm behind him as she kicked his leg out from under him. She spun and added her weight to the force of the man's body as she drove his head toward the railing of the stairway. The metallic thud of her opponent's head impacting the steel rail was overshadowed by the snap of his neck breaking.

Martin rolled off the man and caught the leg of the bloodied second opponent as he kicked toward her head.

With the officer's leg secured, she rose up, grabbing his neck and driving him against the railing. A kick to the inside of his right knee drove him to his knees.

She grabbed her opponent's hair and pulled his face downward as she landed a knee to his face. Then another. As the officer struggled to remain conscious, Martin pulled a knife from her vest and drove the blade into his temple.

Martin let the man's body fall to the ground as she turned toward the stairs.

Moving to the third floor, she peered through the small window to see several men in the passageway. Halfway down the hallway, two guards were posted by one of the doors.

Martin was planning her next move when alarms began to blare across the building's announcement system.

Someone must have found one of her victims.

"Fuck," she cursed, pulling a grenade from her vest and tossing it down the passageway. She took cover behind the wall next to the door as she awaited the blast.

Martin's eardrums popped from the concussion but she was prepared and burst through the doors into the carnage she'd caused.

Smoke filled the passage and debris drifted to the ground as Martin leveled her rifle at a soldier trying to push himself to his knees. A burst from her rifle tore into is body, knocking him back to the ground. She swung her rifle to the left and pulled the trigger again when her sights landed on a bloody soldier trying to raise his rifle with one hand. Her round slammed into his head, leaving a splash of red on the wall behind him.

As she rushed forward, she turned back to her right just as another soldier burst from the cover of a doorway. She rolled forward as he fired and rose to her knees to send a burst into the soldier. Jumping to her feet, she shifted toward her left and fired again as two soldiers ran from the center room. Both fell.

Martin moved quickly to the entrance of the center room and took up a position at the doorway as another soldier rushed from the room. She fired point-blank into his temple and he crumpled to the floor.

Martin sensed movement behind her and dropped to one knee as she spun toward the threat. Rounds tore into the wall above her head as she took aim and knocked another soldier to the ground.

Turning back toward the entrance, she let her rifle hang from its harness as she pulled the torn body of a dead solider to her. With a grunt, she hefted the body off the floor and pushed it into the entrance.

Gunfire exploded and Martin leapt into the room behind the cover of the dead soldier.

She brought her rifle to her shoulder and swung the barrel across her field of fire. Her sights centered on a man with a riot gun and they both fired. The man's body twisted and fell to the floor, Martin letting out a groan as small pieces of shot tore into her left leg. She swung back around the room just as another man rose from behind a large desk.

Her sights landed on his chest but just as she pulled the trigger she shifted her aim, sending a round into his shoulder. The man fell behind the table and Martin rushed forward, leaping on top of the table.

Ignoring the pain in her leg, Martin leveled her weapon on the man. He looked up toward her, his teeth clinched in pain.

"You," he grumbled. "I should have figured Stone wouldn't have the guts to do it himself."

"You're gonna be dead either way."

"Is that Stone speaking? Or you?"

"That's vengeance speaking."

"Then do it, bitch," grunted Maxa as he pulled himself into his chair. "Do what your master can't."

Martin lowered her rifle and sent Maxa toppling from his chair with her boot.

He hit the floor and turned toward her. "Do it!" he shouted.

Martin pulled a knife from her belt and jumped from the desk as Maxa rose to his knees.

"So you want to fight," he added as he stood, reaching for a pistol shoved into his belt.

Martin stepped forward, grabbing Maxa's arm. With a grunt, she drove her knife through his bicep, pivoted as she jerked the blade from his body, and sank it into his ribs.

Maxa staggered forward and Martin caught him, slamming him onto his desk on his back.

"Wait!" he pleaded. "Wai—"

Pinning him against the desk with one arm, she slowly pushed the blade into Maxa's abdomen. He let out a heavy groan as she twisted the blade. "Think about the pain you've caused so many," she said slowly, a calm rage boiling inside her. She pulled the blade from his body only to ease it into his torso again. "Every woman you penetrated..." She twisted the blade. "...think of how they felt."

Maxa let out another moan, but could no longer speak. He stared up at her, helpless.

She pulled the blade from his stomach again. "Women like my cousin." Martin shoved the blade into his lower stomach again. "Maybe it felt like this..." She ripped upward with the blade, slicing open Maxa's torso.

He let out another weak grown as blood began to pool in his mouth.

Martin crawled onto the table, straddling Maxa's eviscerated body. She leaned in until she felt the last, raspy breaths of Maxa's life on her face. "Fuck you," she growled, sliding her blade across his throat.

Movement at the door caused Martin to look up.

Two soldiers stood at the entrance, their weapons leveled at her. They froze, seeing the blood-soaked Martin straddling what was left of Maxa.

Martin rose to her feet, standing on the desk with Maxa's blood dripping from her blade...and most of her body. "This is going to happen to *all of you*," she said slowly, pointing toward Maxa.

A burst of gunfire erupted from the hallway and the two soldiers fell to the floor.

Martin stepped down from the table as Thay entered the room.

"So it's done," he said, unfazed by the scene in front of him.

"No," replied Martin. "All of them die."

"What happened to—"

"My cousin...Maxa took her..." Martin paused as the vision of Aria's blood soaked face flashed in her mind. "...she's dead," she growled.

Thay nodded in acknowledgement. "Then they all die."

Martin stepped past Thay and picked up the riot gun resting next to a dead soldier. She checked the rounds status: seven. "Follow me."

Martin reached the door and dropped to her knees to peer outside. She heard Thay's rifle explode as she pulled the trigger of her riot gun. Her shot sent a surprised soldier's body crashing against the opposite wall.

Rising to her feet, she rushed toward the stairway to her right. She dropped to her knees at a run and slid past the wall at the doorway, firing again. A soldier fell to the floor as Martin's shot disintegrated his left knee. She pivoted, sending a second shot into his chest. Jumping to her feet, she fired twice through the door and then rushed through.

Martin slammed the butt of the riot gun into the jaw of a wounded solider and brought it to her shoulder as she saw two more soldiers halfway down the first run of stairs. Martin's shoulder absorbed the recoil of the riot gun as her last round tore through the chest of the first soldier.

Dropping the empty gun, Martin grabbed the top rail and leapt from the upper level of the vestibule.

She crashed into the retreating soldier, knocking him to the ground. Martin rolled off the soldier and slammed against the wall of the mid-level landing. Absorbing the impact, she grabbed a knife from her belt and leapt toward her opponent as he rose to his knees.

He aimed a pistol toward Martin but she kicked the soldier's left arm against the wall and swung her blade upward. As the knife sank into the man's lower jaw, she heard Thay's rifle sound off and turned to see another soldier tumbling down the stairs below her. Bringing her rifle to her shoulder, her sights landed on a man stepping through the door. The man's head snapped backwards as the bullet impacted his forehead. Martin, sensing Thay beside her, rose to her feet and moved down the stairs to the first floor access. Pushing the door open, Martin saw a short pathway to her right. Above the passage was a medical symbol.

"The exit's this way," said Thay, pointing toward the long passageway in front of them.

"I'll meet you outside," replied Martin, "when I'm done here."

As Thay loped down the passageway, Martin turned down the hall.

She stopped at the only door in passageway; a powerful kick sent it flying open.

Her sights came to rest on a man in medical garb.

"Stop!" he shouted, standing in the center of four rows of beds.

Martin scanned the room and noticing no other threats. "Who are you?"

"I'm the doctor," stammered the man. "There are no combatants here."

"And who are these men?" asked Martin, waving the barrel of the rifle toward the full beds.

"These men have been wounded...they are no threat."

"Fighting for Maxa?"

"This is a medical bay for his officers that have—" The doctor froze as Martin drew her sword. "What are you doing?"

"Get out," said Martin flatly as she stepped toward the first row of beds.

"You can't do this," pleaded the doctor. "These men are—"

"Guilty."

"Please," begged the doctor. "Don't do—"

Martin stopped and turned toward the doctor. Her gaze locked on him as he attempted to muster a look of defiance.

"Get out," she repeated with a calm that did little to hide the fury in her soul.

The doctor lowered his head and walked to the door. He stopped at the exit and turned toward Martin. "You'll pay for your sins…in this life or the next."

"And they'll pay for theirs' tonight," replied Martin as she walked toward the first bed.

***

"Come in!" shouted Orion over the comms circuit as she raced the transport through the forest-covered valley, hugging the ground. She'd received the recall signal fifteen minutes earlier but hadn't received any other communications from Martin or Thay. "Damn it," she cursed, seeing smoke on the horizon. Orion activated the transport's two guns as she called again. "Come in!"

The transport flashed over the last hill and the camp came into sight. Smoke billowed from a three-story building in the center of the camp; the left side of it had already collapsed. A water tower lay on its side and an inferno raged from what had been fuel tanks. "Fuck," mouthed Orion as she brought the transport to a hover and scanned the area.

There were too many bodies scattered across the ground to count.

"Martin! Thay!" she yelled into the radio.

Banking the transport in a slow circle, Orion only saw more devastation. She activated the radio again. "Mart—" She steadied the transport as Martin and Thay came into view. "What the hell happened here?"

"Ready for pickup," answered Thay.

Orion settled the transport onto the charred ground and opened the access door. Idling the engines, she released her harness and rushed toward the troop compartment. Orion stopped when she saw Martin and Thay.

Martin's uniform was covered in dirt, soot, and blood. Her face was blackened from the same mixture. With only the white of her eyes standing out, Martin reminded Orion of the forest demons her grandfather had told her about as a child. "Are you okay?" asked Orion.

Martin returned a blank stare. "It's done."

She turned and sat.

"Martin?"

"She's okay," said Thay as he sat across from Martin. "She just found out who she truly is today."

"And who's that?"

Martin looked up toward Orion, the intense white anger of Martin's eyes chilling the pilot's bones.

"Death."

Chapter 3

General Vispa sipped from his glass of fifty-year old whiskey as he sat at his private table at the Primus Two club.

"More whiskey, General," asked the woman half his age sitting next to him.

"No thank you...uh..."

"Sari," said the woman, reminding Vispa of her name.

"Of course, Sari," he replied with a smile.

Tonight was Vispa's weekly 'staffing' meeting, the night everyone, including his wife, knew was his night to sample the newest, most expensive recreation girls in the city. It was also his chance to unleash all of the rage he held for Astra Varus upon the women willing to take the extra pay...and punishment.

Two men approaching drew Vispa's attention away from Sari's chest.

"Senators," he said. "How can I help you?"

Senators Varo Quextus and Marcus Zetia were both in their early forties and from families that only publically supported Astra's move for power. They had to be up to something.

"General," said Quextus. "It is good to see you."

Vispa returned a vacant stare.

"May we buy you a drink?" asked Zetia.

"I do not think that would be good for any of us," replied Vispa. Astra's spies and informants were everywhere.

"Come now, General. Allow us to pay our honor for your service to the Republic…I mean Empire," said Zetia.

"And most importantly to our leader, ProConsul Varus," added Quextus.

Vispa let out a sigh. "Very well." He turned toward Sari. "Leave us."

"Yes, General," she replied, rising from the table.

"But," continued Vispa, grasping her hand. "Return in five minutes." He glanced back toward the Senators. "That will be all the time we need."

"Of course, General," she said with a smile before walking away.

"What is it that you two want? You know that I will not give you any information regarding the ProConsul." He lowered his glass. "And to ask would raise suspicion as to your loyalty."

"We only want to salute your service as we said," said Quextus.

"And to give *you* some information," added Zetia.

"And what would that be?" asked Vispa, leaning forward.

"Do you know that the ProConsul gets a report through Senator Marcus Sarius from each of the girls you spend time with?"

Vispa leaned back against the couch at his table and laughed.

"First, I wonder why you have been looking into who reports what to the ProConsul."

He watched, noticing a wave of concern pass over Zetia's face.

"And secondly, of course I know this…do you take me for a fool?"

"Of course not, General," replied Quextus. "You would not have been able to retain so much support from the military commanders, nor stay in the ProConsul's good graces if you were."

"What do you want?" demanded Vispa.

"But did you know that the woman with you tonight will only tell Sarius what we want her to tell him?"

"What are you talking about?" Vispa knew Sarius was one of the ProConsul's puppets and that fear of angering Astra Varus kept everyone in line. He leaned forward again. "You know that is not possible."

"It is, General," said Zetia. "We just had to find something she wanted enough to overcome her fear of the ProConsul's wrath."

Vispa laughed. "And what is that?"

"That is our business, General," replied Zetia. "But it is true."

Vispa looked up as Sari returned to the table.

"May I join you?" asked the tall, voluptuous raven-haired woman.

Vispa motioned for her to sit.

As she sat, he felt her hand run along his inner thigh. "Have they told you that you can trust me?"

Sweat began to form on Vispa's forehead. He leaned closer to the Senators.

"What is this about? Tell me before I have you both—"

"Listen, General," said Zetia. "We know Astra Varus is too powerful to challenge now."

"But someday...in the future," added Quextus. "She will become distracted, or a weakness will show itself."

"And you will be one of the first to see it," said Zetia.

"I will not betray the ProConsul," he said slowly, staring into Zetia's eyes. "I have sworn my oath to her."

"Was not the ProConsul supposed to represent the will of the Senate?" asked Quextus.

"Not this ProConsul," snapped Vispa. "And now you will tell me the true power is the people?"

"Ha," chuckled Zetia. "The people are sheep and sheep need shepherds."

"And they have one in the ProConsul," replied Vispa.

"They have a wolf pretending to be a shepherd," said Quextus.

Vispa glanced around the club.

"Don't worry, General," said Zetia. "When Sari speaks with Sarius, she will tell him…"

"I will tell him," said Sari, "that the Senators bought you a drink to honor your service and that, while they may have attempted to test your loyalty to the ProConsul, you rebuffed them and sent them away with a stern warning that you would be watching them."

"See, General," said Quextus, turning toward Sari. "You should head up to the general's room and prepare yourself for him."

Sari turned toward Vispa and smiled before again leaving the table.

"This is a very dangerous game you are playing," warned Vispa. "If the ProConsul—"

"She will not," interrupted Zetia. "So once a month or so, you will spend time with Sari. She will tell you any information we have for you."

"And you can pass information to us from her," added Quextus.

"I don't know about this."

"Just head up to your room and enjoy the girl, General," said Zetia. "Then decide."

The senators rose from the table.

"You may find that having someone to share all of your frustrations with…or on…to be very satisfying," said Quextus before the two walked away.

As the men disappeared into the crowd, Vispa swallowed the last of his drink and looked toward the stairs at the back of the club leading to the rooms reserved for men like him.

Rising from his chair, Vispa made his way up the stairway and to his room.

He opened the door.

Standing in front of him was Sari, but her raven hair was now blonde and she wore a replica of the gown Astra had worn for her last public speech.

"General Vispa," said Sari, "for the rest of the night, you will call me ProConsul."

Vispa stood silent, a mixture of anger and arousal washing over him.

Sari stepped toward Vispa, letting the gown fall to the floor.

"So, general," she said. "Give you ProConsul what you have wanted to give her all this time."

Sari let out a groan and fell onto the bed as Vispa landed an open hand across her face.

Vispa moved to the bed, looking down on her as she slowly turned her face toward him.

Her cheek was bright red from his blow but a bloody smile was painted across her face. "Yes, General," she said as she looked up at him. "Make me pay for the way I have talked to you...how I have humiliated you. Show me the man that you are."

A smile came to Vispa's face as he raised his fist.

***

"Did the electron spin message get out?" asked Akota Major Tama Sand as she coated her wounded leg with coagulant.

"No, Major," huffed Lieutenant Whisper, checking the base's electrical grid. "We lost power to our priority message center when the attack started. We're on emergency power only."

Major Sand looked around the dimly lit control station before letting out a long, frustrated breath. She turned to her left. "Sergeant Valley, any word from the defense forces?"

"No, Major," answered the Scout Ranger. "I've lost comms with all defense teams."

"And the Ranger squad?"

"No contact, Major. All teams are silent...it's just myself and Privates Eaglebow and Sage."

"Damn it," cursed Sand. "Lieutenant, prepare a long-range emergency broadcast message." The rattle of gunfire

45

and an explosion outside of the control station drew her attention. "Quickly, before we're out of time."

"Ready to record, Major," reported Whisper.

"Authenticate message priority, Urgent. Code Fallen Sparrow, repeat Fallen Sparrow," she ordered. Sand then activated the recorder and spoke:

"To all Akota and Confederation units, this is Communications Station *Rainfall*. Station was attacked at 0640 Standard Time. Size of force unknown. Status: Propulsion: Inoperative. Defenses: External at 50%. Spin and Normal Communications: Inoperative. Crew casualties: Estimate 75%. Defense force casualties including Ranger Squad: 90%. Unable to defend station. Attack force not identified by intelligence databases, most likely Elite Guard of platoon strength or greater. Base commander has been killed, Executive Officer Major Sand has assumed command. Will commence self-destruct sequence at..." She looked at the clock above her control panel. "...0730 Standard Time."

Another explosion rocked the control room, followed by the sound of bullets ricocheting off the blast door.

"Send it, Lieutenant," ordered Sand, with a slight crack in her voice.

Sand drew her sidearm and took a deep, calming breath. Communications station *Rainfall* was manned by a crew of 150, a 20-man security detachment, and had recently been augmented by ten Scout Rangers. The force that had taken the station had done so with no warning and decimated their defenses in under an hour. As far as Sand could tell, Lieutenant Whisper, two electronics techs, and three Rangers were all that was left. If there were more, it didn't matter; once they finished the destruct sequence, everyone onboard—and hopefully the attackers—would evaporate in the explosion.

"Message out!" reported Whisper.

"Initiate the self-destruct seq—"

An explosion rocked the room and gunfire erupted all around Sand.

***

Sierra leapt through hole caused by the breaching blast. Still mid-air, she centered her rifle on an Akota lieutenant and fired. She hit the ground and rolled forward, letting her rifle swing to her side as she drew two swords from their sheaths on her back. The sound of her men's rifles echoed in her ears as she kicked a rifle from one of the Ranger's hands and drove a sword through his throat.

Sierra let out a growl as a bullet tore into her thigh but she shifted her weight and swung with all of her might, ripping the sword from the Ranger's neck and laying open the second Ranger's chest. Pivoting again, she drove the sword in her left hand through the temple of the Ranger as he fell. The blade tore through the other side of the Ranger's skull and embedded in the metal deck with a *clang* and a spray of sparks.

Spinning to her right, she drew her pistol and fired a round into the stomach of a startled Akota major. As the major fell, Sierra looked toward the last remaining Ranger.

One of her men had him pinned to the bulkhead.

"Mine!" she shouted as the neuro-med capsule embedded in the base of her skull injected adrenaline and cortisone into her body. Walking toward the Ranger, she felt the nano-neutrophils flowing to her wound as the coagulate serum flowed through her circulatory system.

Stepping in front of the Ranger, she looked into his eyes.

The Akota sergeant, his face twisted in anger, stared back defiantly.

She looked down to see one of her men slowly pulling himself erect with a wound to his abdomen and thigh.

She looked back toward the Ranger and took a deep breath. His scent was one of a warrior. The hair on the back of her neck rose and her mouth began to salivate even more. "You injured one of my men."

He glared at her but did not answer.

"You injured one of my men," she repeated, this time in perfect Akota.

"Let me go and I'll do more than that," replied the Ranger. "And I'll have a good death."

Sierra smiled. "Let him go," she ordered to her men. "Draw your knife," she said quietly, "and I'll give you your good death."

The Ranger pulled a knife from his vest.

Sierra dropped her sword and waived the man toward her. "Let's see what you've got."

The Ranger rushed forward.

Sierra pivoted as the Ranger thrust the blade toward her chest, allowing his arm to pass. She grabbed his wrist and stepped inside of his body, slamming her boot against the inside of the Ranger's right knee.

The Ranger fell to the ground with a grunt and rolled away from her, the knife still in his hand.

"Come on," growled Sierra.

The Ranger let out a roar and slashed at her with his knife.

This time he found his target, embedding the blade in Sierra's shoulder.

Sierra let out a grunt as she grabbed the Ranger's arm and sent a powerful blow crashing into his jaw. Before the Ranger could react, Sierra drove his arm behind his back as she crashed her foot into the back of his good knee. She released a growl that drowned out the Ranger's groan as she pulled hard and twisted on his arm.

The snap of ligaments shot through the room and she dropped to her knees and wrapped her left arm around the top of the Ranger's head. "Here's your fucking good death," she said calmly before opening her mouth wide and sinking her powerful canine teeth into his neck.

Sierra closed her eyes as the salty warmth of his blood filled her mouth and flowed down her cheeks. Sensing the Ranger's heart stop, she opened her eyes and stood. "Is the officer still alive?" she asked, her face painted in blood.

"Yes, Commander," replied one of her soldiers kneeling next to Major Sand.

Sierra picked up her sword and walked over to the body of the first Ranger she'd killed. Placing her boot on the neck of the Ranger, she pulled the other blade from his skull. Sheathing her weapons, she turned and walked toward the Akota major. "I'm guessing you're not going to give us your password."

"Go fuck yourself, Guardsman" spat Major Sand, gritting her teeth through the pain.

"Cute," replied Sierra as she pulled the Ranger's knife from her shoulder and dropped it to the deck. "We're not the Elite Guard...we're something different," she smiled, allowing her canines to show.

"Commander!" reported one of her soldiers standing by the panel where Lieutenant Whisper had stood, "they haven't started the self-destruct sequence yet."

"Well that takes care of that," replied Sierra as she drew her pistol and fired a bullet into the major's forehead. "Alright Sergeant Ball, let's get the data upload going," she ordered. "Lieutenant Kawal, contact the frigate and have them send out the transports."

"Yes, Commander," replied both men in unison.

"Lieutenant O'Neil, casualties?" she spoke into her communications link.

'Three wounded, meds automatically deployed for all. They are fully operational, Commander,' reported the lieutenant. 'All twelve accounted for and standing by for orders.'

"Very well, Lieutenant," replied Sierra. "Search the ship...no survivors."

'Roger, Commander,' came over the link.

"Are you in, Ball?" she asked.

"We're into the facility's comms history, Commander. Encryption override is successful."

"Excellent, Sergeant," replied Sierra as she wiped the blood from her cheeks with her sleeve. "Run a full system search for the names Tyler Stone, Emily Martin, or anyone from her team in any communications."

Chapter 4

Tyler Stone sat cross-legged on the floor of his quarters, playing with Octavius. Since the failed attack on Alpha Humana, Stone had focused on supporting Mori's recovery and getting to know his son. Luckily, the Humani must have been hit hard enough to not take advantage of the failed assault.

Other than the on-going fight between the Akota and the spread of the Word in the Dark Zone, things had been stagnant enough for Stone to remain on Luta-tunkan while Mori healed. Martin and Thay had also taken care of Maxa. From what Stone could tell, the mission had not only removed the threat of Maxa but had brought Martin and Thay closer to some sort of understanding of one another. Although Thay had left to visit his clan in Iroqua territory, Stone hoped the two were now closer to being friends than enemies.

But even while he watched Octavius crawl across the floor, Stone's happiness was tempered by the fact that he knew Astra Varus would do anything to get him back—no matter how many lives it cost.

A buzzing green light notified him someone was outside. Stone rose to his feet and activated the door to his room.

A smile came to his face when he saw Emily Martin standing at the entrance.

"Permission to enter, sir?" she asked, standing at attention.

"Come in, Emily," he replied. "And no need for the formality. We're not in the Guard anymore and you're not under my command."

Martin stepped into the room. "Just because we no longer fight for the tyranny of the First Families doesn't mean we can't honor the Oath, sir," she replied. "They'll never be able to take that from us...and as far as me being under your command..." she continued, extending a data pad.

Stone took the pad. He let out a laugh as he read the orders. "I see you've been given the rank of major in the Terillian Confederation."

"I could give two shits about that, sir," said Martin. "Keep reading."

Another chuckled escaped Stone. "And you've been assigned to my staff."

"If you approve the orders," said Martin.

Stone scrolled to the bottom of the orders and pressed his thumb over the blank square at the bottom. The data pad beeped and the words approved flashed over the orders. "Who else is going to take you?" he said, joking.

"No one," replied Martin flatly. "Absolutely no one."

"Well I'll never turn my back on you," he replied. "You're stuck with me."

"Promise me," replied Martin, her eyes showing a vulnerability Stone had rarely seen.

"Emily?"

"Promise," she repeated, almost pleading.

He looked into her eyes. She needed him to answer.

"I promise."

Martin broke their shared gaze, looking toward Octavius. "How's he doing?"

"He's doing well. The doctors say he is developing well but…"

"What is it, sir?"

"I know I'm going to have to leave him soon," he sighed.

"The life of a warrior, sir," replied Martin.

Stone let himself fall back into the chair behind him. "What if we didn't need any more warriors?"

"I don't understand."

"Do you ever think what it will be like when we have peace…what we will do?"

Martin guffawed. "Peace?"

"Yes. Peace."

"Peace is nothing but a lie told by tyrants and cowards," replied Martin. "There will always be conflict…and death."

"That's a pretty bleak future," replied Stone. "If that's what you actually believe."

"It's not what I believe; it's reality. When have you seen true peace?"

"But there's always the hope—"

"As long as two animals, let alone humanoids, remain on the same planet, there will be war." She paused. "Hell, even if one is left, they will be in conflict with plants, the weather...everything."

"So no peace? Ever?" He began to feel sorry for her.

"The strong always dominate the weak," she replied. "And that matters more than good or evil...good and evil are a matter of perspective."

He could see her body tense.

"Strength is tangible...real," she continued. "The eagle kills the rabbit. Is the eagle evil? The lion kills the deer. Is the deer somehow nobler than the lion because it isn't aggressive? And man kills everything, including man. All of these things are a matter of strength, not good and evil."

"That's very Akota of you," replied Stone.

"No," laughed Martin. "That spiritual crap is a bunch of bullshit. Life is hard. It's full of challenge, struggle, and death...but if you're strong enough, maybe victory and survival."

Stone took Octavius into his arms and let out a sigh. "When I look at Octavius, I can't help but hope for a day when that isn't true." With another sigh, he placed in back on the floor to play.

"Well, sir," replied Martin. "You can hope all you want." She paused as she knelt down, placing her hand on the boy's head. "Until then, you'd better raise him to be strong…"

Stone could tell Martin's thoughts were drifting to a dark place.

"…and a fighter."

"Maybe." He didn't know who to feel sorry for more— Martin because of her dark view of mankind or him because she was probably right.

"And you need to raise him Humani," added Martin, her gaze locked on Stone again. "You can't let these people turn him into an animal worshiping pagan…you must raise him Humani."

Stone didn't know how to answer. He hadn't even thought of how he would raise Octavius. "I just want to raise him to be a good man."

"Then teach him to be a strong man unafraid to fight for what is right."

"But what is right?" asked Stone.

Martin pressed her hand against Stone's chest. "What feels right in here," she answered.

Again, he looked into her eyes. "Sometimes it hard to know."

"Then follow the Oath," she replied. "That's what you taught me."

Another flashing light drew his attention and he looked over to the communications panel at his desk.

"I'll get it, sir," replied Martin, activating the link. "Marshal Stone's quarters."

'There is a priority message from Shirt-Wearer River,' came a voice over the link.

"Roger," replied Martin as she turned toward Stone. "It's one of the Shirt-guys…they want to talk."

"I gathered," replied Stone. "And it's Shirt-Wearer."

"Yes, sir," said Martin. "I'll excuse myself," she added, turning toward the exit.

"Stay where you're at, Major," directed Stone. "You're on my staff now."

Stone touched an icon on his screen and Shirt-Wearer River appeared.

"Uncle," replied Stone. He saw Martin roll her eyes and he shot her a quick glance. "Major Martin is now on my staff and is here with me."

"Very well, Marshal Stone. How is In'o—" River paused, realizing he'd almost used Mori's Akota name with Martin in the room. "…Ka-itsenko Skye?"

"Slowly improving, Uncle." Stone knew the Shirt-Wearers were aware of Mori's status and that River was only displaying a social courtesy.

"This is good to hear. We are anxious to have her return to service."

"Yes, Uncle; we all are."

"I'm not," mouthed Martin with her back turned to the communications panel.

Stone again gave her a quick glance of disapproval and returned to River. "And the reason for your call?"

"You have a new assignment, Marshal."

Out of the corner of his eye, he saw Martin focus on the panel. Her interest was now peaked. "What is it?" she asked, unable to hold back.

"As you know, we learned from Ka-itsenko Skye that Port Royal's support of the Humani is much deeper than we believed. We did not want to take action prior to the attack on Alpha Humana, the Gateway Station, and Dolus. But since that operation has…ended, we have decided to deal with them."

"And how do you plan to do that?" asked Stone.

"That will be up to you, Marshal," replied River.

***

Gunnery Sergeant Mack sat alone at a corner table tucked away in the back of the dark Port Royal bar.

He glanced around the bar before taking a drink of his whiskey. The alcohol warmed his body as it ran down his throat and he thought back to the mercenaries that had tried to kill him weeks earlier:

"Why?" demanded Mack, holding the barrel of his pistol against the temple of the last merc left breathing.

"Fuck off," cursed the mercenary, grimacing from his many wounds.

"No need to play the hero," replied Mack. "You're a businessman, not a warrior...so let's make a deal. Tell me who sent you and I'll let you go."

"Right." The merc's laughter was cut short by another spasm of pain. "Not likely."

"A Marine always keeps their word. I will let you go."

"Fine," grunted the man. "It was a ghost contract but the routing codes were Humani governmental codes."

"Humani?" huffed Mack. "Impossible."

"It's true," coughed the merc.

"Who? What Humani?" asked Mack.

"I don't know. It's just an account stream...but whoever it was really wanted you and the rest of your team dead."

"The rest of the team?" After word of the attack on Alpha Humana, the team had scattered in Port Royal at the order of Lieutenant Plaxis and were told to wait for word from Martin. 'Did Plaxis know something the others didn't?' wondered Mack.

"They're all dead," replied the merc. Between bounty hunters, contract mercs, and Elite Guard, they've all been eliminated. "Except you."

Mack's head began to spin. "Why?"

"I don't know...I just do what I'm paid for."

"Sorry you don't get to collect on this one...asshole," grunted Mack as he increased the pressure of the barrel against the merc's temple. "

"But you said—"

The crack of Mack's pistol cut the merc's plea short. "I am...I'm letting you go to oblivion."

Mack took another drink, again scanning the room. His eyes focused on two armed men as they entered the bar. He knew instantly they were bounty hunters.

He exhaled heavily before finishing his drink. Setting the empty glass on the table, he rose and meandered toward the exit in the rear of the bar. Stepping outside, he positioned himself against the wall and waited.

In a few seconds, one of the men stepped through the door into the alleyway.

Mack grabbed the man's arm and a handful of his hair. He twisted his torso and slammed the man's face against the brick wall with a grunt. He spun around as the first man fell, deflecting the pistol aimed at him by the second man and landing a powerful blow to his opponent's jaw. As the man's head snapped to the right, Mack crashed his boot into the man's knee and drove him to the ground. Holding an arm extended, Mack grabbed the back of the man's head and forced him to look upward. "Who sent—" He paused, realizing the man was too dazed to response. "Damn it," he cursed. "I—"

He heard footsteps rushing toward him and spun to meet the threat.

***

Sierra, already airborne, drove her knee into the Marine's face before he could react. As the Marine tumbled backwards against the wall, her feet hit the ground and she swung her right leg into his chest.

Mack let out a grunt as her boot impacted his chest but he wrapped his arms around her leg. Sierra felt his hold tighten and pushed her body into the air with her left leg, straddling his neck, and slammed her elbow into his temple. The man staggered and Sierra drew a knife from her vest, driving it downward toward his chest.

Just as the blade was about to penetrate his chest, the Marine released his hold on her right leg and blocked her attack. Stepping forward, he gripped her wrists tightly and threw her body forward over his shoulder. Still in the air, Sierra extended her legs and tightened her stomach and legs just before they hit the ground. Her feet impacted the ground and she instantly pushed back, kicking her right leg backward and crashing her foot into the Mack's skull. He again released his grip and Sierra pushed herself to her feet, leaping toward the Marine again.

But he had recovered quickly and caught her mid-air.

She tightened her body as he slammed her against the wall.

Letting out a grunt, she shifted her body as he swung at her. Sensing the air from his punch as his arm flashed past her face, she wrapped her right arm under his and interlocked it with her left as she jumped onto his back. With her arms locked into place around his head and extended right arm, she swung her legs around his waist and overlapped them as she tightened her choke hold.

She felt him stagger but then rush backwards, slamming her against the wall again. Absorbing the blows as he repeatedly crashed her into the wall, she focused on her choke hold and he soon stumbled and fell to one knee.

Sierra unwrapped her legs from her opponent's torso as he fell. She released the choke hold and grabbed his right wrist with both hands, extending his arm at a 45 degree angle from the ground. Letting out a growl, she shifted her weight and brought her left knee crashing into his shoulder blade as she jerked his arm backwards.

The Marine let out a grunt as his ligaments snapped.

Sierra shoved the Marine forward onto the ground and repositioned herself as he rose. As the man stood, she stepped in close, wrapping her arms around his waist and forcing his left arm behind his back. She lowered her shoulder to get low on his torso and pushed upward, lifting him into the air. Once he was off the ground, she rushed forward and slammed him into the wall with his arm pinned behind his back. With her shoulder pressing against his chest, she felt his left shoulder snap and pivoted to toss him to the ground again. Stepping away, she let the Marine—now with both shoulders shattered—stand.

Now she would talk.

"Where—"

The Marine rushed her, swinging his right leg flying toward her left side.

She braced herself and absorbed the blow with a grunt as she caught his leg and drove her right foot into the side of his left knee. The Marine's knee buckled and he fell again.

When he hit the ground Sierra stomped down on the side of his right knee with her left foot. Pulling hard on his right foot, she fell backwards bending his lower leg toward her. Again, the alley exploded with the crunch of ligaments and tendons.

"Now," she said, rising to her feet again. "Time to talk."

"Who…what the fuck are you?" cursed Mack as he tried in vain to push himself off the ground.

"Interrogations don't work that way," replied Sierra. "You're the one that will be answering the questions."

"Then you might as well just kill me now," grumbled Mack. "Because I'm not telling you shit."

"Where are Martin and Stone?" she asked, ignoring his declaration.

"What?"

She could see the confusion painted across his face. "The Traitor and former Paladin Martin?" she said softly as she knelt beside his wrecked body. "Martin turned on her people and you were part of her team…so that makes you a traitor."

"No," he grumbled. "It can't be."

"No. It can't be," she replied, mimicking his denial. "Then why are you lying there all broken and about to die?"

"It has to be a mistake."

"Don't lie to me. Where are Stone and Martin?"

"They were working together?" he said, thinking aloud.

"You really don't know anything, do you?"

"I'm a Marine. I follow orders and serve the Republic and the people."

Sierra laughed. "You had no idea what she was up to? This Martin must be something," said Sierra aloud. "I'm going to enjoy killing her."

"You must let me speak to someone. This has to be a mistake."

Sierra rose to her feet and drew her pistol.

"I've served my people honorably. I don't deserve this."

"You may have served your people," replied Sierra as she leveled the pistol at Mack's head. "But you have failed to understand two things. "First, I serve the ProConsul and she trumps the people …and we all deserve it."

The blast from her pistol rolled down the alleyway.

"Come on out!" ordered Sierra and three of her men stepped from the shadows.

Sierra looked up from Mack's body to her men. "He didn't know anything."

"What are your orders, Commander?" asked Lieutenant Tramble.

Sierra's jaw clinched in frustration. She wanted so bad to literally sink her teeth into the famed warrior Emily Martin and the Traitor Stone. "We'll report back to the ProConsul."

"Yes, Commander," replied the lieutenant.

"Do you have a question, Lieutenant?" she asked, seeing a quizzical look on his face.

"Yes, Commander…if I may?"

"Ask."

"Why didn't we just shoot him from the shadows or overpower him with numbers?"

"Oh that," answered Sierra, her canines flashing against the light. "Where would the fun have been in that?"

Chapter 5

Stone looked at the orbital map behind Admiral Crow as he spoke, studying it intently while listening to the Admiral's brief in the crowded staff room.

"Port Royal defenses consist of fifteen to twenty corvettes, cruisers, and frigates—mostly last generation that shouldn't be too much of a problem for our assault force. The major threat will come from their attack craft and orbital defenses. Best estimates are that they possess up to 3000 fighters and attack craft."

"What are the capabilities of these aircraft," asked a commander from the crowd of Commanding Officers and Regimental Commanders.

"Ranging from ancient hulks up to some advanced models," replied Crow. "Our biggest problem will be their orbital guns. We have confirmed reports that the Association has been scavenging main batteries from wrecks of ours and Humani capital ships throughout the Dark Zone. They have installed these as defense batteries across the moon."

"Even if some are old…" asked a captain from the front row. "…fighters and attack craft in numbers that large can swarm a battleship or carrier and take it out. Especially if one of the untold number of Association spies has already warned them of the possibility of attack."

"Yes," added another captain. "How do we know we're not already compromised?"

Admiral Crow swallowed hard. "We've taken all possible precautions...but that must be a contingency we are prepared for..."

A wave of murmurs passed over the group, unsettling Stone.

"We must get our fighters launched immediately after the assault jump and get them in position to keep their fighters clear of our big ships."

"What are the expected casualties for the fleet?" asked Stone.

"Fifteen percent, Marshal Stone," replied Crow. "And that does not include possible casualties inflicted on assault troops before they disembark my ships."

Stone exhaled heavily. "General Vae?"

"Yes, sir," replied Vae as he stood.

As Vae walked toward the center of the briefing room, the map behind him transitioned from an orbital map to a sectionalized topographical map of the Port Royal area.

"Our landing zones are designated as—"

"What are the casualty estimates for the assault forces?" interrupted Stone.

"Five percent before departure from the fleet and fifteen to twenty percent during the assault, Sir."

Stone closed his eyes, doing the gruesome math. "So 3,000 fleet casualties and 12,000 from the assault force?"

"Yes, sir," replied Vae and Crow in unison.

"15,000 infantry and half that in ship's crew for thirteen Association Councilmen?"

Vae and Crow stood silent, understanding his question was rhetorical.

Stone glanced over to Martin and Orion, sitting just to his right. He let out another forced breath. "That will conclude the brief," ordered Stone. "Everyone is dismissed except Admiral Crow, General Vae, Major Martin, and Flight Commander Orion."

More murmurs.

"You heard the Marshal," barked Vae. "Dismissed!"

"That big brain of yours isn't overthinking things again is it, sir?" asked Martin, leaning forward from her chair as the room emptied.

"Probably," he replied.

"Was there a problem with the brief, sir?" asked Vae.

"Yes," answered Stone as he saw the last of the officers leaving the room. "I'm not going to lose 20,000 men for thirteen Port Royal assholes."

"Sir," interjected Admiral Crow. "Then how are we—"

"Is the mission to occupy Port Royal or to break the power of the Association?" asked Stone.

"Aren't they one in the same?" asked Orion.

"They don't have to be," replied Stone. He stood and walked to the sectional map of Port Royal. He pointed toward the administration polis. "Do we need three battlegroups and two divisions to remove these people from power?"

"No, sir," replied Martin, a smile coming to her face.

"What are you talking about, sir?" asked Vae.

"I need both you and Admiral Crow to reconvene this brief tomorrow and we will run through it exactly like we have. After the brief, direct your COs and Regimental Commanders to brief their divisional and company level officers."

"But, sir," replied Vae, concern showing on his face. "That might pose a significant security issue given the possible depths to which Association spies have infiltrated our ranks."

"It might," replied Stone. "So be sure to tell them secrecy is key."

"You want the Association to find out?" asked Crow.

"I do."

"But why—" Vae paused. "You will use the threat of a large-scale assault as a diversion."

"They'll be expecting a hammer and we'll use a needle," replied Stone.

"Or more like a hammer instead of a sledgehammer," said Martin.

The group turned toward her.

"What," she replied. "I'd rather be called a hammer than a needle."

"So will we or won't we be attacking Port Royal?" asked Admiral Crow.

"You're planning on getting the old gang back together again, aren't you?" asked Orion.

"Yes," replied Stone. "If we can get the Association to think they know the day and time of the attack, they'll most likely concentrate their forces and be looking outward instead of toward internal security. The Council, at least most of them, will probably meet in a central location for security. Under these conditions, a small tactical team can enter Port Royal and make a quick assault on the administration polis. If we are fast and lucky, we can take them out without a large number of casualties."

"It will be risky," replied Vae." What if it fails?"

"Then we use the hamm—" He paused, glancing toward Martin. "...sledgehammer."

"I like it," said Martin.

"Who will be on the team?" asked Vae.

"We'll need people who are familiar with the layout...Major Martin, Orion—"

"Katalya and Magnus," added Orion. "And I guess we'll take Rickover."

"Consider Staff Sergeant Shara as volunteered," added Martin.

"We will need more," added Stone.

"Ki'etsenkos?" asked Orion.

"If we can get them," replied Stone.

"Guess you're talking to the Shirt-guys again," said Martin with a chuckle.

"You know that's not what they are called," said Stone, his lips curled in a frown.

"I wasn't laughing at that, sir."

"Then what is it?"

"Just picturing you telling Ki'etsenko Skye you're going on a real, old-fashion mission and she can't."

"Sir?" asked Vae. "You're not going to risk yourself on this mission, are you?"

Martin laughed again. "Don't worry, sir. You can tell her I've got your back."

***

Stone stood outside the rehabilitation room, his hand poised over the activation pad.

He took a deep breath and activated the door.

As the door slid open, he saw Mori. She had an exoskeleton brace attached to her waist with hydro-bionic braces running the length of her newly-grown leg.

She took a labored breath.

"Good," said a medical tech standing next to her.

Mori's face grew red with pain and determination as she grimaced after taking another step. She exhaled forcefully and moved again.

She let out an audible moan.

Stone's heart ached. Even though she was recovering quickly given the extent of her injuries, she still had some painful months ahead of her.

She looked up and saw Stone. "Wanna race?" she said, a forced smile coming to her face.

"I should," replied Stone. "I'm pretty sure this would be my only chance at beating you." He paused. "It'll be no time until you're 100 percent again."

"I think I could beat—" Mori fell to the ground mid-step, letting out an ear-piercing cry.

Stone rushed forward as the tech knelt down to help her.

"I'm okay!" she grunted, shoving the tech's arm away and raising her hand to Stone. "I can get up on my own."

Stone's body tightened, wanting to help, as he watched Mori slowly push herself off the floor.

Almost panting from the pain, Mori let out a grunt as she stood erect. "There...see."

"She's doing well, Marshal," reported the tech to Stone. "At this rate we expect she should be walking on her own in a few weeks and back to full duty in three standard months."

"Two," replied Mori as she took two painful steps and let herself collapse onto a nearby medical chair. When her legs bent, she let out another groan. "Two and a half."

"That's what I wanted to talk to you about," said Stone as he pulled a nearby chair next to Mori and sat. "The Port Royal mission—"

"As long as the date doesn't move, I'll be ready," she interrupted.

"Well, there's been changes," replied Stone.

"What?" asked Mori, grimacing as she involuntarily shifted her leg.

"We should get you in your bed so you can rest, Ki'etsenko Ino'ka," interjected the tech.

Mori's head snapped toward the tech. "I'll lie down when I'm ready." She turned back toward Stone. "What changes?"

Stone paused, looking at the tech. He had almost forgotten he was there. "I'll take care of her for now," he said to the tech, politely hinting for him to leave.

"As you wish, Marshal," replied the tech before exiting the room.

"Talk," demanded Mori.

"It's been decided that a special operations mission will be undertaken instead of a full scale assault."

Mori's eyes sparkled briefly but quickly grew pale. "When?"

"Six standard weeks."

"That's bullshit!" cursed Mori. "I should be leading such an attack...are the Shirt-Wearers aware?"

"They are."

"Then who did they pick to lead it?"

"I'll be leading the mission," replied Stone.

"You...you're a fucking Marshal."

"Am I not capable?" huffed Stone.

"That's not what I meant," grumbled Mori. "I know you are...but why would they pick—" She paused, taking in a deep breath and nodding. "You volunteered."

"Well, yes. I—"

"Let me guess, the mission was your idea?"

"It was," he replied. "A special ops mission has the same, if not better, chance of success and could save the lives of thousands of our troops."

"And it just has to be in six weeks."

"We're still acting as if the full scale assault is going to happen with the assumption that Association spies will get word. Going earlier gives us an advantage."

"And keeps me out of the fight," grumbled Mori.

"You know that's not the reason," replied Stone. "If I could have you there—"

"I know," interrupted Mori. "It just sucks."

"I know. But you'll be back out there soon."

"Who's on your team?"

"Orion will be our pilot, so obviously Rickover will be there. And—"

"Let me guess, your little pet Martin will be going?"

"Why wouldn't she?" asked Stone. "She's—"

"Never mind," replied Mori. "Who else?"

"Your sister and Magnus volunteered. As did First Sergeant Shara."

"Another Humani," interjected Mori.

"Another Humani with experience," replied Stone, trying to ignore Mori's dislike for his men. "And I have requested two Ki'etsenko."

"So everyone but me."

"Ino'ka, I—"

"I know," she interrupted. "Just let me be pissed about it." She let out a frustrated breath. "Who did they give you?"

"Captain Littledove and Sergeant Crowdog."

"They're good," replied Mori. "But all Ki'etsenko are. Thay has just returned from his people...you should contact him." She paused. "Maybe he can keep your minion in check."

"I—" He paused. It wasn't worth the fight. "I'll contact him."

"Well," continued Mori. "I guess that will give me and Octavius some quality time together."

"Yes. I have let Mrs. Vae know to expect you once you're out of the rehab facility. General Vae's wife has agreed to keep him until I return."

"So he is staying with Humani?" asked Mori with a scowl.

"Where else would he stay?" He paused. "I mean…" His stomach tightened—he hadn't thought about how Octavius would complicate things. "You need a few more weeks here, then you'll be training…I just…it's not that I…"

"Stop," interjected Mori. "I'm not asking to be his mother—" Now it was Mori who paused. "I didn't mean I don't want to be part of—" She sighed. "What I am asking is why doesn't he stay in the Clan Mother facility while you're on missions?"

"What?" asked Stone.

"The Clan Mothers facilities are where our children go when their parents are deployed. Clan mothers volunteer their services and ensure the children are taught our traditions and customs—just as their parents would have. Men also volunteer so that the children understand they are always part of the greater Akota family. The position of the Clan Mothers is as honored as that of our best warriors."

"A group of strangers?" asked Stone.

"Not strangers, Magakisca. Fellow Akota."

"What is wrong with Vae's wife watching her? She has two children and volunteered?"

"She's not Akota," replied Mori.

"Well neither is Octavious." He saw the frustration and anger on Mori's face. "What I mean is he's not only Akota. Do you expect him to learn nothing of his Humani culture?"

"There is no Humani culture," growled Mori, another wave of pain shooting through her leg. "It is a fabrication of the Xen to—"

"It was—is—real to me," interrupted Stone, his own anger growing. "I was made by that culture. Martin was—"

Mori guffawed. "Martin. Of course."

Stone clinched his jaw. She just wouldn't let it go. "You're going to have to realize that even if I fully embrace Akota culture part of me will always be Humani."

"Why do you insist on holding on to the lie that is Alpha Humana?" She grunted as she repositioned and another wave of pain washed over her.

"Because it's part of me!" he shot back, almost yelling. "Being Humani seemed to be good enough for you that night on November 14. It was a Humani that rescued you from that prison on—" He stopped.

He'd gone too far and knew it.

"It wasn't a fucking Humani that saved me!" she shouted as tears began to flow down her cheeks. "It was you! Not a Xen slave…You did those things because at your core you're Akota…" She took another breath. "Why are we…why is this so hard?"

Stone closed his eyes momentarily to calm himself. "Ino'ka, I didn't come here to upset you. I—"

"Well, you failed there," interrupted Mori, looking toward the floor.

"I'm sorry. And I do want Octavius to learn the Akota ways." He placed his hands on her cheeks, slowly raising her head until their eyes met. "And I can't think of anyone better to teach him than you." He rubbed a tear from her cheek. "And I'll look into these facilities for future missions." He made sure she was looking into his eyes. "But for this mission, Octavius will stay with the Vaes."

Mori let out an exasperated laugh and looked away.

"But," he added, turning her back toward him. "I want you to see him as much as you can…and teach him."

"Sure," she replied.

"Seriously. I'll speak with Mrs. Vae; she will not interfere."

A forced smile came to Mori's face. "I'll visit him."

"Thank you," he replied. "I have to go brief the others."

"Fine...but someday," she replied, placing her hands on his face, "you're going to need to figure out who you are."

***

Martin felt everyone's eyes on her and Shara as they entered the briefing room. As she looked over the group, she paused on each face.

Orion—good...no great pilot. And a bitch.

Orion returned Martin's gaze for a moment and then with a scowl turned away.

Rickover. Weird...just weird.

Katalya and Magnus—weird and creepy.

Then she turned toward Thay.

Martin formed a forced smile as she stared at the Iroqua warrior. She'd once thought they would someday finish the dance started on that riverbank. But the mission to kill Maxa had changed that. They may never be friends, but as much as she hated to admit it, Thay might have understood her better than anyone.

Thay gave a small nod, acknowledging their gaze.

Next she turned toward the other two Akota Ki'etsenko. "Who are these jerkoffs?"

"These 'jerkoffs'," replied Orion, turning back toward Martin. "Are Ki'etsenko and should be shown some respect."

81

"Oh, excuse me," gasped Martin in the Akota language she was quickly learning. "It's my honor to meet two more noble warriors," she said in a high, mocking voice as she bowed. "Where's your makeup, girls?" she added, returning to a deadpan tone.

"I see you haven't changed," grumbled Thay stepping next to the two warriors.

"Why would I?" she asked.

"This is Captain Littledove and Sergeant Crowdog," replied Thay.

Martin took a step toward Thay and the others. "Ladies," she said as she curtsied.

"This is the Red Wolf so many have spoken of?" asked Crowdog. "Doesn't look like much to me."

Martin had grown use to every Ranger seeing her as a potential trophy to mount on their wall. "Wanna see what I got?" asked Martin, gripping her sword.

Crowdog's body tightened.

Out of the corner of her eye, Martin saw Shara place his hand on his pistol.

"Stop!" shouted Thay, stepping in between Martin and Crowdog. "Now is not the time. We have more important things to do."

"You're right," grumbled Martin, relaxing her stance. Martin smiled at Thay again before looking over his shoulder to wink at Crowdog. "Lucky day," she said.

"Can we just sit quietly and wait for Stone?" offered Thay.

"No problem," replied Martin. "We'll be right over here in the no-makeup section," she added as she pointed to the opposite wall.

"Fine," replied Thay.

"Fine," mocked Martin as her and Shara moved toward the other end of the room.

"They really don't like you," declared Shara.

"Apparently I'm not good at making new friends," said Martin.

"No shit…" replied Shara. "…with all due respect."

"Fuck off," retorted Martin.

"And what is that Red Wolf shit?"

"Apparently if you kill enough of them, they give you a name," she said with a smile turning back toward Crowdog and letting herself fall into a leaning position against the wall.

"This is going to be an interesting mission," said Shara.

"Just wait—" Martin saw Stone enter the room. "Attention on Deck!"

Standing like an oak, she saw Shara come to attention next to her in her periphery. And every Akota in the room turned in surprise.

"At ease," ordered Stone. "And you don't have to do that anymore," he added.

"But we're going to, sir," replied Martin. "Because that's what the Guard does," she added with a glance toward Orion. "We respect our leaders."

"On that note," replied Stone. "Let's get started."

***

Stone didn't feel like refereeing an argument between Martin and the Akota so he started right into the briefing.

"If successful, this mission could save thousands of lives," he said as he activated the 3D hologram map of the Port Royal layout. "Has everyone read the threat briefing?"

Martin raised her hand.

"Major," said Stone, acknowledging her.

"Sir. So...how are we getting in...and more importantly, how are we getting out? I'm guessing they're locked down tighter than a First Family virgin."

"From what we can tell, access to the polis are still pretty open," replied Stone.

"The Association still needs to make money so they'll keep everything but the administrative polis open," added Orion.

"And the admin polis is going to be the problem," continued Stone.

"They'll have the maintenance areas more secure, won't they?" asked Katalya.

"Probably," replied Stone. "We used that option the last time we were there."

"Then what's your plan, Marshal Stone," asked Sergeant Crowdog.

"A little subtlety, a big diversion, and some really big math," answered Stone.

"Well that doesn't sound complicated at all," said Shara to Martin, just loud enough for Stone to hear.

"It's not," interrupted Rickover, hearing Shara as well. "Stone has discussed the plan with me."

Everyone turned toward Rickover and then Stone.

"Did I mention the math part?" added Stone, trying to defend why he'd spoken to Rickover before the others. "Orion, do you remember the atmo jump on Kilo 2?"

"That was awesome," replied Orion. "Wait—do you want me to try that again?"

"Yes," replied Stone. "But this time I want you to jump from the docks at the market polis to the security area leading to the administrative polis and then from there to the Association Council Hall."

"Two fucking atmo jumps of just a few kilometers? No fucking—" She paused. "Rickover, what the hell did you tell him?"

"I just told him it was theoretically possible to make short range atmo jumps with an acceptable risk."

"And what is acceptable?" asked Martin.

"Seventy-three percent chance of success," answered Rickover.

"And the other twenty-seven percent outcomes?" asked Martin again.

"Not successful," replied Rickover.

Murmurs passed over the small group.

"So what's your plan, Stone," asked Thay, redirecting the group.

"We have to be fast for this to work so I had Rickover look over the data and do the math to see if it was possible," continued Stone. "We dock in the market polis and Katalya and Magnus exit and move toward the security access on the opposite end of the polis. No uniforms or weapons."

"What about these?" asked Magnus, displaying his canines.

"Those you can take," replied Stone with a smile. "Once you're within 100 meters of the security zone, drop a nav beacon and get out of the way."

"We can use the beacon and the software I'm designing to make a more precise jump code so—"

"You do realize that once I leave the docks, I'll need to get above the highest structure and still be below the atmospheric barrier then go to full power at a hover to make this happen?" asked Orion.

"Yes," replied Rickover. "You should have about ten meters to be clear."

"Oh, that much," replied Orion.

"That's part of the calculus that goes into the 73 percent," replied Rickover. "We already discussed that."

Orion raised her hands in the air and leaned back in her chair. "My bad, please continue."

"Thank you," said Rickover. "Once the first jump is complete."

"First," guffawed Orion. "Never mind...keep going."

"Once the first jump is complete, we will blast through the door using the ship's guns and then pickup Katalya and Magnus."

"Why do we have to blast through the doors?" asked Shara.

"The walls extend to the atmospheric barrier," answered Orion.

"Will taking out the wall affect the barrier stability?" asked Martin. "I'd rather not do this in atmo-suits."

"Again, part of the 73 percent," replied Rickover, frustrated at the need to repeat himself. "I already said I calculated the risks."

"Go on, weird math guy," said Martin.

"Yes," continued Rickover. "Once through, we'll do a jump directly to the Association Council Hall."

"That's like sixty kilometers," said Orion. "I can make that at full atmo speed in less than two minutes."

"But we can jump there in a few seconds," interjected Stone.

"Okay," said Orion, "you know I'm up for just about anything but do you know what a short range jump at atmo like these are going to feel like?"

"Probably like getting punched in the gut," replied Stone.

"Try having your stomach punched out of your body and landing about—I don't know—sixty kilometers away."

"But can it be done?" asked Stone.

Orion raised her hands in the air again. "If Rickover says the math works then I can do it. You bastards just better not eat anything before because I don't want your lunch all over the ship."

"Good to know," replied Stone. "No eating before." He changed the 3D image to an orbital map. "Admiral Crow will help us out with a diversion that should draw off some of their forces. Five battleships will jump into Port Royal's orbit;

that will be our signal. They are going to go after some of the batteries outside of the polis boundaries. Two carriers will also jump to make them think a landing may occur. Hopefully that will keep most of their defense forces busy long enough for us to get a head start. He won't stay on station very long, but it should be enough. Once we're at the Hall, we'll go in with two teams and sweep the building."

"Is this a search and destroy op?" asked Littledove.

"If we can take any Council members, we will," answered Stone. "But our primary goal is to put an end to their control of Port Royal. If we have to take them out, that's we do."

"Do you think we'll get all thirteen of them?" asked Thay. "Won't some be at their residences or someplace else?"

"That's a possibility but our intel tells us there is a high probability of most of the members being there."

"If one or two are not?" asked Martin.

"Hopefully they're all there," replied Stone. "If members are unaccounted for and data is missing, word will get back to the Xen and Humani that the Association is a security risk. Once that happens, the Xen, and definitely Astra Varus, will lose faith in them." He paused, contemplating Astra's response to losing her most valuable connection in the Dark Zone. "She might even finish off the rest of the survivors herself."

"So how do we know who the council members are?" asked Katalya.

"We have positive IDs on seven of them…their info will be uploaded to your mission files. The rest…just look for someone hiding behind the guys with guns."

"And how long do we have to pull this off?" asked Orion. "While you guys are playing scavenger hunt, I'll be fighting off ground and air-to-air fire."

"About ten to fifteen minutes," replied Stone.

"Oh, that's all," laughed Martin. "That will be about five to ten minutes too long for a transport or an alpha."

"Hopefully Admiral Crow's diversion will help…but I think you should be okay with the ship we are giving you."

"What do you mean?" asked Orion, her interest peaked.

"Well," interjected Rickover. "Always wanted to design a ship and since the Shirt-Wearers are supporting this, they gave me all the resources I need," he continued as he stood and changed the image of the orbital map to one of a ship. "Introducing *Hydra* II."

"What is that?" asked Orion. "It looks like a flying box."

"*Hydra* II," continued Rickover, "is being designed as a special operations insertion craft. If you notice the normal mode exterior structure, you'll see it looks very plain—similar to typical freighter and passenger craft used by mid-to-upper lever companies and organizations in the Dark Zone."

"Looks like a storage container," added Martin.

"You want me to fly this?" huffed Orion. "And you have the balls to call this flying brick *Hydra* II?"

"If you will wait," grumbled Rickover. "As I said, this is the normal mode—designed to not draw attention. But when *Hydra* II is shifted to combat mode…"

Rickover selected a button and the image of the ship transformed as two swept wings extended from the blocked frame and two external engines extended from the aft end, enclosed by armored plating.

"Shit," declared Orion as the ship continued to morph.

"Now," continued Rickover, "in normal mode the weapons systems, combat electronics, search and fire control sensors, and self-defense systems are secured and undetectable to external scans until combat mode is selected. When this is done, the superstructure is reconfigured to support high speed combat in both space and atmospheric environments. Armament includes four plasma cannons, two 30 mm rotary guns, four self-defense pods—each carrying six tubes of Viper anti-missile and aircraft weapons. Its search and fire control systems are the same as our Type IV Foxtrot fighters. Propulsion systems include two small modular reactors, four solid state emergency and auxiliary power supplies with one standard week of backup power, and a solar sail for tertiary power."

"Holy shit," interrupted Martin.

"The comms suite includes spin message capability as long as one of the reactors are online and the armor is similar to our main hover tank but reinforced with durumite plating."

"How fucking heavy is it?" asked Orion.

"Heavy," replied Rickover, "But the weight is offset by an improved reactor design that increases thermal efficiency from .6 to .8 and utilizes a recovery system that captures heat from electrical and ambient losses and returns .14 of these losses to the solid state supplies."

"I fucking love you, Rickover," exclaimed Orion. "I've got pilot wood like you wouldn't believe right now...where is it?"

"It's being built...should be ready for its first flight next week," replied Rickover.

"So," continued Stone. "If we're okay with the ship—"

"Oh, we're okay," said Orion.

"Then after our time is up, we'll get back onboard and make the push back to the security gate and then jump to Admiral Crow's fleet. Once we dock on his flagship, the entire fleet will jump." He paused to let the group absorb the information. "Any questions?"

Martin raised her hand?

"Martin," acknowledged Stone.

"So just to summarize…we're gonna take ten people up against the entire Port Royal defense force using 'theoretical'," she said making quotation marks with her hands, "calculations on never-before-tried short range atmo jumps on a prototype ship then grab some assholes and get out?"

"Pretty much," replied Stone.

"Now that's my kind of mission," replied Martin.

Chapter 6

"Where are they?" demanded ProConsul Astra Varus as she rose from her throne.

Still looking toward the marbled floor, Sierra spoke. "ProConsul Varus, the information from the communications station provided little information on the whereabouts of either of the traitors...and the Marine knew nothing."

"Then why have you returned if you have not completed your mission?" growled Astra. "Every moment you fail me is another moment my Octavius is with those savages."

Sierra dropped to one knee, still bowing her head. "I am sorry to have displeased you, my ProConsul, but I felt it necessary to return based on the information we obtained at the station."

"What information, Commander?" asked Astra.

"We found communications indicating a large scale attack on Port Royal will occur in the coming months."

"An attack on Port Royal?" interjected General Vispa. "That will take a lot of resources... why would they attack a neutral?"

"My job is not to ponder politics, General," replied Sierra. "It is only to do as the ProConsul wishes."

"I do not care about Port Royal, Commander," said Astra as she descended the small stairway from her throne to the main floor. She placed her hand under Sierra's jaw and gently directed her to stand. As Sierra rose to her feet, Astra tilted the warrior's head so that their eyes met. "Your only assignment is to find Octavius and kill those that took him from me."

"Yes, ProConsul," replied Sierra. "And I have never lost focus on my mission. I believe if there is an attack on Port Royal that Stone and senior Scout Rangers will be involved...possibly the traitor Martin as well."

"Continue," replied Astra, releasing her hold on Sierra's jaw.

"I returned to gain your permission and gather the rest of my company before leaving for Port Royal. I plan to arrive before the attack—"

"We should warn the Association," interrupted Vispa.

"No," replied Sierra. "The ProConsul's orders are to retrieve Octavius and kill the traitors. I will have a higher probability of doing that if we allow the Akota to occupy Port Royal."

"While that may be true, Commander Skye," replied Vispa, his revulsion for Sierra and the other modified warriors evident, "but the Association is a neutral by treaty and—"

"General," interrupted Astra. "We both know the Association are no neutrals."

Vispa glanced toward Sierra and then turned back toward Astra.

"You may speak freely, General," said Astra. "I trust her more than I do you."

Vispa took a deep breath, absorbing the insult. "But we must find a way to prevent the Association members from being captured and interrogated by the Terillians. They know too much about..."

"About the virus and Dolus," said Astra, showing Vispa her trust in Sierra. "If—" Astra paused. Her heart ached for her son and burned for revenge against Stone and Martin...but she could not let the Terillians pick the brains of the Association members.

"The secrets they know," continued Vispa. "They could—"

Astra, still in thought, raised her hand to silence Vispa.

She turned toward Sierra. "Kill them."

"ProConsul?" asked Vispa.

"Commander Skye," continued Astra, ignoring Vispa's question. "Once the attack begins, and before the Terillians land, I want you to kill all of the Council members."

"Yes, my ProConsul," replied Sierra without hesitation. "As you wish."

"But the—"

"Fuck Port Royal," snapped Astra, interrupting Vispa again. "They have served their purpose. We can find other organizations in the Neutral Quadrant to assist in obtaining captives and we already have the workforce in place for continued construction on Dolus. We can also find other sources of revenue. She paused in thought. We will start by increasing the levy on the middle classes. We will call it a loyalty…no, a patriot tax to support the war." She stepped in close to Sierra. "My sweet, deadly pet," she said, running her hand through Sierra's jet black hair. "You must kill them all. Not one of them can speak a word to the Terillians."

"It will be done, my ProConsul," replied Sierra. "And then I will bring you your son and the heads of the traitors Martin and Stone."

Astra smiled. "Once the Dolus army is ready and the virus is unleashed on the Xen and the others," she said, with a glance toward Vispa, "you, my loyal little lioness, will lead my armies of conquest."

"As you wish, my ProConsul," replied Sierra.

"But for now, Commander," continued Astra, "go to Port Royal and do what you do best."

***

"And you're convinced this plan will work?" asked Shirt-Wearer River.

"It has just as good a chance as the full-scale attack...with a lot less lives on the line." Stone wasn't sure why he'd been called to see the Shirt-Wearers at such a late hour, or why they were asking about a plan he'd already proposed to them over a standard week ago.

"This is good news, given the report from *Rainfall*," added Shirt-Wearer Shadow.

"The communications station?" asked Stone. "What news?"

"It was taken four standard weeks ago," answered River.

"I hadn't heard of Humani or Doran ships being in that sector."

"It wasn't attacked by fleet," said Shirt-Wearer Wolf. "We believe it was a platoon of Elite Guard. They must have used remote insertion with exposure suits. The first warning of their presence was multiple hull breaches. They took out most of the shipboard defenses before their frigates appeared."

"They also killed a squad of Rangers attached to the station," added River.

"A platoon?" Stone found it hard to believe even the Elite Guard could pull off an attack like that.

"We just received the long-range report *Rainfall* sent just before it fell," said Wolf. "It's likely they received information regarding the initial attack plans."

"How do you think the Humani will react?" asked River.

"They might send a force to defend their interests," replied Stone. "But when Astra hears of this, she will see them as a liability...she may try to take them out first."

"Do you think the Humani will solve our problem for us?" asked Shirt-Wearer Falling-sky.

"But that will leave the Humani in control of Port Royal," said River.

"And we will lose the opportunity to get information from any of the Council members...if we can take them alive," offered Stone, his brow furrowed in thought. "So we must accelerate the plans even more."

"When can you be ready?" asked River. "Your original plans were for a mission five weeks from now."

"My team can be ready in three standard weeks, which will allow us to be on station in four."

"Will Admiral Crow be able to support a week early?" asked Falling-sky.

Shirt-Wearer River began activating screens embedded in his desk. After a few seconds, he looked up. "Both carriers assigned to the mission are in the yards until one week prior. And one of his battleships is on detached duty and won't be able to be on station by then."

"We can attempt to accelerate the carriers," said Wolf.

"We can make the attack with just four battleships," replied Stone. "But at least one carrier would help to keep their defenses focused on a possible invasion force landing."

"Are you willing to make the attack without the carriers, Marshal?" asked River.

"To save thousands and possibly nab a Council member? Yes."

Stone stood silently as the Shirt-Wearers looked at one another.

After a moment, River turned toward him. "The acceleration of your mission is approved."

***

Martin stood outside Stone's quarters.

"Com' on," she said aloud.

The door slid open.

Mori stood in the entrance.

"Oh, it's you," mouthed Martin.

"And of course it would be you," replied Mori.

Martin took a breath. "I'm here for Marshal Stone."

"We'll he's not here," replied Mori. "He's with the Shirt-Wearers."

"What?" Martin knew it must have been urgent if she hadn't been informed. "Why?"

"I don't know, Major," snapped Mori. "I'm not involved in those conversations right now."

"Hmm," said Martin, glancing toward Mori's leg. "Looks like that thing's finally starting to work a little. Bet it still hurts like a son-of-a-bitch," she added with a smile.

"I don't know; how long did it take your arm to stop hurting when I sliced it off."

"Well, mine was a clean cut…but yours…it was all jagged and juicy. Gotta be—"

"He's not here," interrupted Mori, shooting daggers at Martin with her eyes. "So there's really no reason for you—"

"Where's Octavius?" said Martin, leaning into the entrance and looking past Mori.

"I don't see how that is any of your concern."

"That boy will always be my concern," replied Martin. "Where is he?"

"He's with the Vaes," grumbled Mori. "Now it's time for you—"

"Good," interjected Martin.

"And why is it good?"

"It's good for him to be with his own kind."

"His own kind?"

"Yes," replied Martin. "Humani."

"You do realize there is no Humani civilization, right?" asked Mori. "It's just a lie whispered in the ears of fools that were only too eager to listen."

Martin's skin grew hot. "Well my non-existent civilization has been killing people from your real one for generations." By the tightening of Mori's face, Martin could tell she was hitting a nerve. She continued. "And you want to talk about reality? Worshipping animals and the fucking sky? At least—"

"We don't fucking worship them," growled Mori. "We respect them...you know that concept you seem to not understand?"

"Oh, I understand respect...and I give it when it's deserved."

"Why do you hate us so much?"

"I actually don't hate your civilization," replied Martin. "I mean I think you're all superstitious nutjobs...but I don't hate your people." A tight smile came to her face. "Just you...for trying to change him."

"He's just..." Mori paused, her head tilting slightly and her mouth gaping. "You...you're in love with him."

The words were like an explosion in her gut. Stone was her commanding officer; she didn't love him. Not like that...she couldn't. "Fuck you," she spat. "If you can't keep him it's because he's getting sick of you trying to run his life based on your religious bullshit."

"And you're stopping him from becoming the leader he's supposed to be."

Martin laughed. "That's the problem...you think he's not good enough when he's already too good for your scheming ass."

"I should've put a bullet in your brain back on Juliet 3 when you were lying in the mud bleeding out," said Mori in Akota.

"Maybe you should've," replied Martin in Akota with a dry smile. She took a second to enjoy Mori's surprise at her new-found ability to speak Akota. "But you didn't." She stared into Mori's eyes. Those fucking brilliant green eyes—the eyes of the witch that had Stone wrapped up in her spell. Martin really did hate her. "And that's why all those Rangers died on Echo 2."

"You fucking bitch," said Mori through her teeth. She stepped toward Martin but paused, her body spasming as pain coursed through her body. "Those men were..." She looked up into Martin's eyes again. "One day I might just finish what I should have on Juliet 3."

Martin moved closer, her face only centimeters from Mori's. "You already tried that once. But if you want to try again..." She stepped back and readied herself. "I'm ready."

Mori gritted her teeth as another wave of pain shot through her leg.

"Emily!" declared Stone, causing Martin to break her gaze with Mori.

Martin turned to see Stone standing behind her. "Sir," snapped Martin.

"What's going on? What are you two talking about?" asked Stone.

"We were—"

"Major Martin was looking for you," interrupted Mori. "I was just wishing her luck on your upcoming mission."

Martin's head snapped toward Mori and then back to Stone. "She was..." She paused. Even she knew it wasn't the time. "What did the Shirt-Wearers want to talk about?"

Stone motioned for them to step inside the room. After the door slid shut, he spoke.

"We're going a week earlier," said Stone.

"A week earlier?" asked Mori.

"Why?" asked Martin.

"*Rainfall* communications station was attacked," said Stone. "It was taken."

"So we have to assume the Humani know about the initial plans for the attack on Port Royal," posed Mori.

"We'll need to get at the Council members first," said Martin. "Astra will go after them."

"That's what I told the Shirt-Wearers. They still don't get the way Humani think."

"You're telling me," replied Martin with a quick glance toward Mori. "They probably never will."

"That's because the Humani don't even know how they think," added Mori. "The Xen have been thinking for them too long."

Martin glowered at Mori. Injured leg or not, she wanted to punch the bitch in the face. But she knew she wouldn't be able to stop there. She took a deep breath. "How did the station fall?" she asked Stone.

"They think it was a Guard unit but they apparently started the attack with a team wearing environmental suits launched from beyond detection range."

"No shit," replied Martin. She tried to think of who would be on that team.

"How many survivors?" asked Mori.

"None."

"Do we have any intel on the team?" asked Martin. "What info do you have on their tactics? How—"

"I think all of that can wait until tomorrow," interrupted Mori, stepping forward and placing her hand on Stone's chest. "It's already late." Mori turned her green eyes toward Martin. "And I'm sure you can brief your subordinate in the morning."

Martin fumed. "Sir. I..." She stopped. She wasn't going to let Mori bait her into a fight. "I'll be standing by at 0600." She started toward the door but stopped. "But if I could have a quick moment outside...it is an issue with Sgt. Shara." She returned Mori's gaze. "It's a Humani thing."

"Sure," replied Stone.

"And we'll continue our discussion someday, Major," said Mori.

"Someday we will," replied Martin.

Martin nodded and stepped outside. Stone followed.

"What's going on with Shara?"

"Nothing, sir," said Martin.

"Then why did—"

"Sir," interrupted Martin. Her heart began to race. "She is bad...no dangerous for you."

"What? I know you two don't—"

"No," pleaded Martin. "She's in your head...making you not think straight. She only cares about what you can do for her fucking destiny. Not about what you need. I—"

"Enough, Major," snapped Stone, his face red with anger. "And I suppose you know what I need?"

"No, sir," replied Martin, stepping back. Even in combat, she'd rarely seen him this angry. "I just—"

"Perhaps you should keep your recommendations to military matters, Major," he said, his face slowly returning to normal. "This is my..." He paused. "This is private."

"Yes, sir," grumbled Martin through her teeth. "I meant no disrespect. I just—"

"Tomorrow, Emily," interrupted Stone. "We will talk more tomorrow."

"Yes, sir," she replied, presenting a crisp salute. "Tomorrow."

Martin stood motionless as Stone turned and entered his quarters.

"Damn it," she cursed as the door slid shut. She looked up toward the ceiling. "Fucking bitch," she mouthed. She had to find a way to get Stone to see what that witch was doing to him. "Tomorrow," she said quietly. "Tomorrow."

***

"Prince Vali," said Astra with a smile. "I am glad you could see me at this hour."

"Your support of my brother King Vali and the naming of Lord General Zorlar in your report to the Emperor has brought honor to our family and made you a friend of the true Doran King."

"It is I who am honored," replied Astra.

Prince Vali nodded. "And what have you asked me here for, ProConsul?"

"I offer to your King the base of Port Royal."

Vali tilted his head. "Is this not the base of your Association allies?"

"They are no longer allies," replied Astra.

"Then why don't you take care of them yourself?"

"I have more pressing matters in other sectors but have also recently obtained information that the Terillians are planning an attack. I cannot let the Terillians gain control of Port Royal."

"This Association must not be very good at playing the neutral."

"As I said, I no longer have need of them."

"And you want the Dorans to take care of the problem for you?"

"I have put things in place to weaken their defenses when you attack in five standard weeks."

"Five weeks," replied Vali in what Astra though was laugh. "Do you now also plan to tell the Dorans when to attack?"

"No, Prince Vali. But in order to take the city before the Terillians, you must do so in five weeks."

"And why would I order my forces into combat for you? You have to know by now the Dorans do not spill our blood needlessly."

"I do, Prince," said Astra. "I can assure you, when you start your attack their leaders will be dead. And then you will have a foothold in the Neutral Quadrant...one the Xen will be unaware of. From there you can gain resources and possibly information on the Siksika and Numinu people that can help you in your struggle with them."

"The Association must have—or know—something you really want to keep from the Terillians."

"And I am sure you have secrets you do not want your enemies to learn as well, Prince."

"Or our allies," he replied.

"Of course. Then we understand each other."

"We do, ProConsul."

"Then I offer Port Royal to your King as a gift from the Humani people."

"And what will be my gift, ProConsul?" asked Vali.

"It will not be the first time you will unwrap it, Hector," replied Astra using the Prince's chosen name, "but I am sure you will find it just as pleasing as the first time," she added as she let her dress fall to the ground.

***

Stone's thoughts wondered as he walked toward his office. Mori had remained tight-lipped about the conversation between her and Martin. He knew the two didn't like each other…he even knew why. But he had no clue what to do about it. Every time the two were together around him, he felt as if he was being pulled apart by two mountain bears.

Turning the corner to his office he saw Martin leaning against the wall at the entrance.

"Sir," she replied as she snapped to attention.

"Emily?" he replied.

"Sir…you said we would talk this morning."

"Yes, of course." He'd hoped she would have dropped the issue. But it was Emily Martin. "I really don't think—"

"Sir, if I may?"

"Emily, I shouldn't have snapped at you but I can't—"

"Just…damn it," cursed Martin. "Just fucking listen to me…" She paused. "Sir."

Martin was mouthy and opinionated but had never directly challenged him. "Go ahead."

"I'm am truly sorry and meant no disrespect last night," said Martin. "I've never tried to understand your personal life. You've been my commander and it's my job to follow your orders. And that's been good enough for me…until now."

He really didn't want to have this conversation. "Emily. I—"

Martin raised her hand to silence him. "You're going to let me finish…or find another Chief of Staff."

Martin was not one to toss around ultimatums she wasn't willing to carry out. "Fine, Emily. Speak your piece."

"You have taught me how to lead men and…" She paused, taking a deep breath.

He could see tears begin to well up in her eyes. "Emily?"

"I'll never forgive myself for thinking you were a traitor against our people."

He placed his hand on her shoulder...he didn't know what else to do. "Emily, it's not—"

"Please," she said, shrugging his hand from her shoulder and looking toward the floor. "I know a lot of people don't..." She let out an awkward chuckle. "...nobody likes me. I'm a pain in the ass."

"Emily—"

She looked up into his eyes. A resolve had replaced her fragility. "But you know there's no one you can count on more in a fight."

"I do," he replied. "I—"

"If you can trust me unconditionally in battle, then why won't you trust me when I tell you that woman is not good for you?"

He took a deep breath. "She showed me the truth about the Xen. I wouldn't be alive if it wasn't for her...she's been my anchor."

"She told an enemy what she knew to be the truth for her own benefit...a truth that has made you question everything..." She exhaled hard. "...even yourself. You've risked your life for her as much as she has for you...if you're not careful that anchor will drown you."

He couldn't hold back anymore. "Damn it," he cursed, slamming his fist against the wall. "I can't keep being the referee between you two...I don't have the energy."

"I just don't want you to lose yourself in your attempt to fight the Xen."

He saw Martin's jaw tighten and felt her hand on his forearm as she spoke.

"And I'm afraid she is going take you away from…" She stopped and stepped away from him, looking toward the floor again. After a deep breath, she looked up. "…away from your people."

"Our people are always in my thoughts," he replied. "And as for losing myself…" His stomach felt tight. "How can I do that…I don't even know who I am." he confessed allowing his own frustrations to boil over. "Am I honoring our people? Am I a traitor? A leader of men or a puppet of the Akota?" He stepped forward and grabbed Martin's arms. "If you are so sure who I am, please fucking tell me because I just don't know anymore."

Martin's eyes locked onto his.

"You are brave, honorable, and should be the true leader of our people," she replied. "You are the one that taught me what it meant to be a warrior, an officer…how to be Humani."

Stone saw the conviction and the pain in her eyes. "I don't know—"

"And every minute you let that Akota fuck with your mind—and your heart—I see it changing you."

112

"I…" He let out an audible grunt full of frustration. "What if it is for the better?"

Martin guffawed and turned her head away from him briefly. "She's…it's not for the better."

"What do you want me to do?" asked Stone, holding his arms out in frustration. "Tell me."

"I—" The look in Stone's eyes told her he didn't want an answer.

"Can you just focus on the mission right now?" asked Stone. "Unless you really mean to resign as my Chief of Staff?"

She stared back at him, her mouth twisted and jaw clinched. "I won't jeopardize this mission," she said with a sigh. "But there will come a day—and it will come soon—that I'll have my fill of watching her destroy the man that our people need you to be."

"Well until that day comes, Major," replied Stone. "I expect you'll do you duty."

Martin snapped to attention. "You know I will," she replied. "And when that time comes—and I do what has to be done—I'll be doing my duty then as well."

He knew exactly what Martin meant…subtly was not her style. "Just make sure the team is ready for the mission." He paused. "And remember…we are all on the same team."

"Yes, sir," grumbled Martin, adding a salute. "Now if I may be excused."

Stone nodded his head.

Martin dropped her salute and stepped past him.

He turned and watched her storm away, her ponytail bouncing with each angry step.

"Son of bitch," he said aloud. He was pissed at her but she had only said things that he'd thought himself on occasion—things he and Mori had even fought over. He glanced back in the direction of Martin as the door to his office opened.

She was gone.

Letting out a sigh, he stepped into his office, walked to his desk, and let himself collapse into his chair. He looked toward the ceiling and let out another heavy breath. Stone closed his eyes for a moment and let his mind drift back to before the war had started, before things were…complicated. His hand tightened into a fist as if he was holding his sword as he remembered the night he recited his Oath for the first time. He began to speak them again:

I will stand strong in the face of danger, for my comrades will do the same

I will be unafraid of death for death comes but once and cowardice is forever

I will go close against the enemy, for my will is stronger than his

I will show courage, for it is the one possession that cannot be taken

I will die with pride, for I am fighting for my lineage and my people

I will face death with joy, for I will become immortal—my shining glory never forgotten

A heavy puff of air escaped his lungs. The words that had always seemed to center him brought no relief. Mori's pressure to change him and Martin's resistance to everything Akota—the Oath held no answers to that problem. At its core, the Oath was meant to center a warrior on duty to their people and the importance of family. But in order for that to mean anything, one had to know what family they belonged to….what people they were part of—in short, one needed to know who they were.

Stone's stomach churned and his head grew light. How was he supposed to lead thousands if he couldn't keep Mori and Martin from wanting to tear each other apart?

"You better figure it out soon," he said to himself as he closed his eyes again.

Chapter 7

Sierra, with Lieutenants Kawal and O'Neil at her side, stood at the entrance to Councilwoman Woodstock's office. She looked over the two Association guards at the door. They were both large with thick beards and strong jawlines that would intimidate most would-be opponents purely on appearance alone. Unlike the other Association members, they wore little leather and brass finish on their uniforms. They were made for practicality, not flash.

She looked into the eyes of one of the guards who returned her gaze with an arrogant confidence. If they only knew her true mission. She let out a small chuckle.

"More of the fucking ProConsul's pets," laughed the guard. "And how is the biggest bitch in the galaxy?"

Sierra smiled, allowing her canines to show. "Now that wasn't nice."

"Oh," replied the guard. "Did I—"

In a flash Sierra was on the guard. She drove him to his knees, grabbing his rifle and tossing it to the ground as Kawal and O'Neil leveled their weapons on the other guard.

Sierra felt the guard start to rise but shoved him back to his knees with a growl. "Now, Port Royal trash," she said through her teeth, "I think you need to apologize for taking the ProConsul's name in vain."

"Get off me!" he grumbled. "Fucking Guardsmen."

Sierra's body tensed. "We're not Elite Guard," she grumbled. She tightened her grip on the guard's shoulder, sending a bolt of pain through his body.

"What are you then?" he groaned.

"The future," she snarled, slamming his body against the wall.

"I…I'm sorry," he relented. "I meant no disrespect."

Sierra shifted her weight and lifted the guard to his feet with one hand. "Do it again and I will drain you and bathe in your blood."

The door slid open and out walked a tall, thin woman in a black dress covered by a leather vest. Her face was pale, made purposely so with makeup, to highlight her raven hair and blue eyes. Her jaw dropped when she saw Sierra had the guard pinned against the wall. "Oh, my," she gasped. "Is…is everything okay?"

"Yes," replied Sierra, releasing the guard. "I was just ensuring your guard understood the importance of showing respect for the ProConsul Astra Varus."

"Yes. Of course," replied woman with a glance toward the guard. "Please forgive him. Our guards are chosen for their physical abilities, not their politics. His pay will be docked."

"I think he understands now," said Sierra with a glance toward the guard. "And besides, you don't change behavior with a pocketbook…you do it with pain."

"Of course," replied the woman, "but don't you think there are many different types of motivation?"

"Perhaps for some." Sierra knew Association members were masters of flattery, deceit, and manipulation. "But make a man cry out in pain and you will see their true self."

"That method would seem to be effective as well," replied the woman as she stepped toward Sierra. "I am Selena Swanson. I am Councilwoman Woodstock's attendant."

Sierra felt the woman's hand on her forearm. "No," she said. "No games."

"Of course," replied Selena, quickly withdrawing her hand. "Let me take you to the Councilwoman."

"Yes." Sierra turned toward her lieutenants. "You two stay with our new friends."

Sierra followed Selena through the doors and into the councilwoman's office. Orchestral music played softly in the background as they walked across the wooden-planked floor to a desk of dark wood and brass.

As they reached the desk, a tall leather chair turned and Councilwoman Sienna Woodstock came into view. Her puffy cheeks turned red as a smile came to her face. "Come, Commander Skye, sit," she said as she rose to her feet. "The

118

ProConsul has told us you would be arriving soon. As usual, any emissary of the ProConsul is welcome on Port Royal."

"Don't worry about the niceties, Councilwoman," replied Sierra. "I'm a warrior, not a politician."

"Of course, Commander," said Woodstock, her smile turning flat. "What can the Association do for you, Commander?"

"You mean for the ProConsul?"

"Yes, Commander. For the ProConsul."

"The ProConsul has learned of a security threat to Port Royal."

Woodstock exhaled. "So the Terillians are going to attack," said Woodstock. "We had heard rumblings and were preparing a meeting with the ProConsul to discuss a request for support in turn for a more favorable trade status with the Humani."

"I'm not here regarding the Terillian assault," replied Sierra. "The ProConsul is making preparations for the attack on this facility."

Woodstock let out a sigh of relief. "That is good to hear. Are you here as part of those preparations."

"No Councilwoman."

"I am confused, Commander Skye. Why are you here?"

"I'm here regarding a specific threat to the Council."

Woodstock sank into her chair. "To the Council?"

"I have been sent to brief the Council and provide assistance to your security forces. The ProConsul is concerned your focus on the coming Terillian attack will only increase your vulnerability to the threat."

"What is the threat?"

"I must brief the assembled Council. Those are my orders."

Woodstock leaned forward and her brow furrowed. "That is highly unusual? As the Head Council Member I can inform the others."

"The threat is highly unusual. And I have my orders."

The Councilwoman activated a panel in her desk and began to flip through files. After a few seconds, she looked up. "It may take a few days to assemble everyone," said Woodstock. "Councilmen Ravenwood and Coppertree are away…" She paused. "…on business."

"Then you should recall them immediately." Sierra leaned forward, placing her hands on the Councilwoman's desk. "This threat is very real," she added, allowing her fangs to show. "That's why I'm here."

Woodstock leaned away from Sierra. "You're one of them."

Sierra stood erect. "I will assign a team to each of the Council members currently on Port Royal…for their safety. I'll also need to see your head of security."

"This is highly irregular, Commander Skye. If you could just tell me the nature of the threat…our security structure is very robust."

"I have told you my orders, Councilwoman," replied Sierra. "And if you want Humani support against the Terillians, you will allow us to ensure the Council is protected…which means my team will provide the protection."

"Of course, Commander."

"And my men will need quarters while we are billeted here," said Sierra.

"Uh…yes," replied Woodstock, "Ms. Swanson will ensure all of your needs are met."

"Excellent." Sierra activated a communicator. "Lieutenant Kawal, post."

Lieutenant Kawal walked into the room and saluted. "Reporting as ordered, Commander."

"Your platoon will be attached to Councilwoman Woodstock."

"Aye, Commander," answered Kawal.

Sierra turned toward Woodstock. "Once all of the Council members have arrived, Lieutenant Kawal will inform me and I will brief all of you on the threat. Are there any questions?"

"No, Commander," replied Woodstock. "And please convey to the ProConsul our appreciation for her continued support."

"The ProConsul is aware," said Sierra.

Sierra turned and exited the office. Once outside she was joined by Lieutenant O'Neil.

"Is everything on track, Commander?" he asked as the two walked down the long passageway leading away from Wooodstock's office.

"Yes, Lieutenant. Pass word to the frigate to send a spin message to the ProConsul. Inform her that the Council should be assembled in a few days."

"And then—"

"We kill them."

***

Astra Varus smiled as she looked across the table toward Prince Vali. She'd forced herself to offer up her body to him, knowing the Doran's were driven as much by lust as by power. At first, the thought had turned her stomach but it didn't take long to find out why Doran's had become so popular in the Recreation Houses. Despite the pleasure Prince Vali had given her, Astra's focus was still on her own goals. "How is your dinner, Hector?" she asked.

"Very good, Astra," he replied. "I believe I have acquired a taste for Humani delicacies."

"Perhaps," she replied with a coy smile. "Then I am sure you will enjoy dessert."

"ProConsul," came a voice away from the table.

"What is it, General Vispa?" asked Astra without turning to see the General at the entrance to the dining area.

"Please excuse the interruption but we have received a message from Commander Skye," reported Vispa. "Her team has contacted the Head Councilwoman and she expects all Council members to be on Port Royal in a few standard days."

"Excellent," replied Astra. "Prince Vali," she turned her gaze back to her diner companion, "is your fleet in position?"

"They are within a standard day's jump of Port Royal, awaiting the command."

"Very good. Once my people have eliminated their leadership, they will wreak havoc with their defenses from inside."

"My brother is very pleased with your offer," replied Vali.

"Well…" Astra paused, turning toward General Vispa. "Is there anything else, General?"

"No, ProConsul."

"Then you are excused."

"Of course, ProConsul," grumbled Vispa.

After General Vispa exited, Astra returned her attention to Vali. "As I was saying, Hector. I am pleased King Vali sees the opportunity Port Royal offers."

Vali laughed. "And he also sees that it will also draw us into direct conflict with the Akota in addition to our current fight with the Siksika and Numinu."

Astra stopped chewing. "I—"

"Don't worry, my dear," said Vali. "I have long argued the need to obtain new territory, wherever it is available. I am assuming this offer—like that of your body—is to serve some need of your own as well."

Astra swallowed hard. He was no fool so she wouldn't play him as one. "Well, Hector. I do believe you are getting something—out of both offers."

"That I am, Astra. And don't worry about me interfering with your plans...at least at this time. The taking of Port Royal will add valuable resources to the Kingdom and specifically my family. The Southern King has been questioned by the nobles about his resistance to supporting Xen requests to expand the war—"

"Requests?" asked Astra.

"We both know what a Xen request actually is, but King Tal is dragging his feet and forcing the North to carry the brunt of effort. The nobles, both North and South, are growing tired of it. Some have even talked of unification of the Kingdoms under one family."

"Which could make you the King of the South," said Astra. She and Vali were from different cultures and subspecies, but they were like minds.

Vali raised his drink. "We all have our ambitions," he replied.

"Yes, we do," said Astra, raising her glass.

"Care to tell me yours?" asked Vali.

"I do not," she replied with a smile. "At least not yet."

"I feel in the end, my dear Astra, we will either become inseparable allies or bitter enemies."

"Is that not true of all lovers," she replied. "But it makes for a much more passionate union."

Vali laughed. "Very true…but I feel our breakup may be more…what do you Humani call it…dramatic than others."

***

"I think you can do better than that," said Councilman Mortimer Coppertree.

Coppertree had spent the last two standard weeks negotiating a mining agreement with the warlord Ibri who controlled a small moon orbiting Tango 8. The moon was rich with titanium and durumite; if the deal could be brokered, then the Association wouldn't have to pay mercs to take it or split the profits with the Akota or Humani.

Ibri let out a groan. "You know I could trade directly with the—"

"You don't want to do that," interrupted Coppertree, "regardless of who you were going to say."

"And why is that?"

"You know you don't want that. Once those bullies get involved you'll find your little world crawling with Terillians trying to cram equality down your throat or better yet, the Humani will just park a battle cruiser in orbit and force you to turn over power to them." He stopped to refill his glass and let Ibri ponder the options he had just presented. "Now is that worth a few percentage points?"

Ibri slammed back his drink. "And what if they show up anyway?"

"Once we have brokered a deal, the Association guarantees little to no involvement in your affairs by either the Humani or the Terillians. Our agreements with both sides allow us autonomy to make such deals…it will be honored."

"Fine," sighed Ibri. "I can use the quick money…"

Coppertree was distracted by a communicator beacon flashing on his wrist. He looked down to read it: 'Message Status: Urgent. Return to PR immediately due to security risks. Under advisement from Humani security team, a full assembly will be required to learn all the details. Return with all haste.'

Coppertree looked up from the message and then toward his security guard. "We must go," he said. "Important Council business."

"Do we have a deal?" asked Ibri.

"Uh…yes. Of course," replied Coppertree. "I will send you the agreement and the first 10% of the payment for your first delivery will be sent upon signature."

"Excellent. I—"

"I am sorry, Mr. Ibri, but I must leave immediately." He turned toward his guard. "Let's go."

Coppertree quickly rose from the table and made his way to the exit of Ibri's villa. Once outside he turned toward his guard. "There is a significant security risk to the Council," he said. "We must return to Port Royal at once."

***

"What is the risk?" asked the guard. He could tell the Councilman was unsettled.

"I don't know. Apparently we are to return for a full assembly of the Council."

"If there is a real threat, why would the Council gather? Shouldn't you disperse?"

"I would think so but apparently a security force from Alpha Humana has arrived on Port Royal and recommended a full assembly before they provide the details of the threat."

"That doesn't…" The guard paused. "And we were alerted of this threat from the Humani?"

"Yes, Dan-Lee," replied Coppertree. "So we should listen."

"We should," replied the Phelan warrior. Dan-Lee knew enough of Humani treachery to know something foul was afoot. But maybe this would be his chance to get one step closer to his revenge against the Ragna family. Although the Elite Guard had waged the genocidal war against his people, it was under the order of the former ProConsul Ragna and it was his lineage that most deserved his wrath. And it would only be sweeter if he could take out a few Guardsmen along the way.

***

Stone watched as Martin illuminated the 3D model of Port Royal. With *Hydra II* into its jump toward Port Royal, it was time to go over the attack one last time. The focus brought on by the start of the mission had been good for him. The last few weeks before he had left Luta-tunkan had been filled with tension. He and Mori fought more than not. Martin had turned into a robot. And the few times the two had been in the same room, Stone could feel the hate between the two radiate like a two stars on a collision course.

"*Hydra II* will be here," continued Martin, "while Katalya and Magnus, designated Wolf—"

"That's original," quipped Orion.

"Designated Wolf," repeated Martin with a cold stare toward Orion, "will move to this security checkpoint and drop the beacon. After the first jump, we'll blast the security gate, pick up Katalya and Magnus, and then jump to here." She pointed toward a location near the center of the Administration Polis. Once we're at the Council Hall, we'll insert in two locations. Team Alpha will consist of Marshal Stone, Staff Sergeant Shara, myself, and Sergeant Crowdog. We'll insert here at the West end. The Akota will provide cover and pickoff anyone trying to get out while the rest of us enter the building and move east. Bravo will be Captain Littledove, Thay, Katalya, and Magnus. Katalya, you will provide cover while the others enter and move west. Hopefully, we'll meet in the middle. From there we'll move to the west and embark." She looked up from the display. "Any questions?"

"Secondary evacs?" asked Littledove.

"Here and here," replied Martin, pointing to two locations on display. "But if we're not in and out fast, it probably won't matter. We expect less than 50 guards at the Hall given the distraction from Crow's fleet, but every minute after they know we're there that number will grow." She turned toward Stone. "Sir," she said flatly.

"The key will be timing," said Stone. "Once we dock, we'll send the signal for Admiral Crow's orbital destroyers to commence their jump. It will take them exactly two standard hours from their staging point. That will give Katalya and Magnus more than enough time to make it to the security gate. We will synchronize time when the signal is sent. Katalya and Magnus, drop the beacon at time 1:50 and move back to a safe position." He turned toward Orion. "When Crow's ships hit orbit, they will open fire on batteries outside of the main city. We will detach from our mooring at 1:58 so they can't lock us down. After the firing starts, we'll make the first jump." He stood from his chair. "Remember, if this mission fails, thousands of our brothers and sisters will die taking Port Royal."

"If there are no more questions...," said Martin. "...we will be entering Port Royal orbit in less than fifteen standard hours. Prepare yourselves."

***

Martin stared at the top of her bunk.

They would be at Port Royal in less than eight hours and sleep eluded her. Her frustration with Stone's tolerance for Mori had begun to affect her performance. And she was sure Stone knew it too. Her father would have told her to do her duty and stay out of her commander's private life. But her father had also kept the biggest secret in the galaxy from her.

Once she'd opened the door to her history with men, her mind ran through the usual list of frustrations. Jackson had torn her heart apart and put it back together so many times...then he died. And then there was Stone. She had once idolized him. But her hero worship had been destroyed when she thought he'd turned on his people. Then, when she found out the truth, her guilt over doubting him had been somewhat tempered by the hopes he would become the man that would someday lead their people out of Xen tyranny.

But that Akota savage had a spell on him.

"Damn it," she cursed under her breath as she slid her legs out of her bunk and hopped onto the deck. 'Time for another late night walk,' she thought as she stepped into her trousers.

She activated the door and stepped into the hallway.

Standing in front of her was Stone.

"Shit," she cursed.

"What?" replied Stone.

"I'm sorry, sir. I just—"

"Can we talk?" he asked.

"Sir, it's late and I just need to get some things off my mind."

"I understand, Emily but this is important," said Stone.

He hadn't called her Emily since their argument outside his office before they had left Akota territory. "Yes, sir," she said.

"We need to fix this."

"I don't understand what you mean—"

"Just stop it," interrupted Stone, almost pleading. "If you have any respect for me at all, you'll drop the attitude."

"Fine," she huffed. "It's not that I don't respect you. I..." She let out a frustrated laugh. "If I didn't respect you I wouldn't be—"

"So pissed at me," said Stone.

"Yes," she replied. "But I don't want to have the same fight again." She lifted head toward the overhead and let out a heavy breath. "I have to focus on the mission."

"I understand," replied Stone. "That's why we need to solve this before we land."

Martin's stomach tightened and she shifted her gaze to the floor. "I don't know if we can."

"I know the trouble between you and Mori is only because you're afraid she is trying to change me to fit her own needs."

She looked up toward Stone. "I do," she said. "If you know, then how can you let her do it?"

"Truthfully?"

"Yes," she exhaled.

"I don't know." He shook his head. "I wish I did…but I don't."

She had never seen him so…lost. "Sir?"

Stone leaned against the bulkhead and put his hands on his waist. "So much has happened so fast.—the news of the Directive and of the First Families' collaboration with Xen." He looked directly into her eyes. "Don't you feel lost now that you know the truth?"

Martin laughed. "I've felt lost my whole life." Her slight smile turned to a scowl as she continued. "Everyone I've ever cared about one way or another has let me down so, honestly, when I found out the truth that was the first thing in a long time that made sense…it justified my hate for them."

"But it was different for me…I knew the First Families had their faults but I believed there was an underlying good in the order of things. When that belief was shattered, I felt empty…and she filled that void."

"But she's filling that void with poison," replied Martin, stepping toward Stone and placing her hand on his forearm. "Don't look to her to center yourself…look toward those of us—other Humani—that are willing to fight for our people."

"I do…but I have feelings for her." He placed his other hand over hers. "And she does want to do what's right for her people…and she thinks the Humani are part of her people."

"Only if they accept her version of what we should become…shouldn't we decide?" She exhaled heavily. "Isn't that the whole reason we're resisting the First Family rule?"

"Yes. And I'm not saying you're wrong, but the conflict…and my feelings for her—"

"Do you love her?" She swallowed hard, her stomach in freefall. Martin stepped away from him. Why did she ask him that?

"I do—I don't know. I thought I did…but now it's just so hard and we fight about the future so much."

"Listen to someone who knows. If it feels too hard, then it's too hard." She closed her eyes. She shouldn't be talking to a superior about these things, but she had to tell him. Martin opened her eyes again. "Do you know how much I wanted it to work with Hugh?"

"I know you loved each other."

"I did…and I wasn't unsure like you are. I felt it in here," she continued holding her hand to her chest. "And here," she added sliding her hand to her stomach. "And we were still doomed to fail." She focused her gaze on him, staring deep into his eyes. "Where do you feel it?"

"I…"

"Probably right here," said Martin, pressing her index finger against his temple. "Stop thinking and feel."

"Maybe you're right," he sighed.

"I am," replied Martin, letting her hand slide down to his cheek before quickly pulling away. "But tonight is not the night to focus on the homefront, sir" she said, refocusing herself. "What would you tell a private worried about matters at home the night before a mission?"

"That if they didn't lock it down and focus on the mission, they would never get back to deal with the problems at home."

"Then you should do the same, sir."

Stone sighed and let a weak smile form. His eyes looked into hers and her stomach tightened again.

"You're right, of course," he said. "Thank you."

"That's my job, sir," she replied, turning her head to break their gaze. "Now you should get some sleep; we've got a busy day tomorrow, what with all the shooting and whatnot."

"Yes, ma'am," replied Stone, giving her a mocking salute. "And thank you."

"Goodnight, sir," she said. "Now go."

Martin waited until Stone turned the corner of the passage before letting her torso fall against the bulkhead and gently bouncing the back of her head off the wall. Her stomach felt like it was floating; she wouldn't sleep tonight. "Fuck," she mouthed. "What are you doing, Emily?"

Chapter 8

Daria Vae read from a book of Humani poetry as she watched Octavius and her son, Marcus, play on the floor. Looking up from her book, Daria saw her husband, General Taris Vae enter the room.

She could see he was troubled.

"What is it, Taris?"

"We are to be deployed soon," he replied.

Daria slowly closed her book. This was not she first time she had heard these words, nor would they be the last. Such was the life of a soldier's wife. But this seemed different.

"For how long?"

"I do not know?"

Daria saw there was more to her husband's troubled look than another deployment. "What is wrong?" she asked.

"Something is not right about this assignment."

"What do you mean?"

"Marshal Stone's entire division is being sent to Echo system to deal with more Followers of the Word."

"Is it the Followers that trouble you?"

"No," replied Vae. "They are fanatics but that is not it."

Daria rose, placing her hand on her husband's arm. "What?"

"They are also sending Admiral Crow's fleet and General Fallingrock's division with Colonel Sand's brigade."

"That is a large contingent."

"It is…but I fear we will still have a long fight on our hands given the size of the forces we will be facing."

"Are more troops not available?" asked Daria.

"They are," replied Vae as he stepped away from Daria and poured a glass of whiskey. "Almost an entire corps is available and not reserved for any pending operations."

Now Daria grew concerned. Her husband had never shared these kinds of details about a mission. "Why can't they be used?"

"I do not know," replied Vae. "Fallingrock was placed in command until the Marshal returns…he also asked for additional forces and was denied." Vae took another drink. "Based on Stone's previous success, the Akota usually deal with the Followers with overwhelming force to help establish and control safe zones and allow the inhabitants to regain a sense of security so they will eventually join us in fighting them."

"But not this time?"

"No. They told Fallingrock the troops were marked for reserve status and not available. He was also told Stone would take command when he returns from his current mission."

"We at least he will be in command instead of an Akota," said Daria.

"Yes. He will be in command of a force insufficient to handle the mission without significant casualties and a long struggle." Vae finished the drink in his hand. "And in doing so, the Akota will also have occupied Stone, our Humani troops, and every single Akota commander loyal to him...except Colonel Skye."

"Really," huffed Daria. "I would think they would have his Akota babysitter attached to his hip...not that she needs an order to do that," she continued with a scowl.

Vae let out a laugh that trailed into a low sigh. "She was promoted to command a regiment, one that is currently available to deploy. But when I asked Fallingrock about her, he said her regiment had 'other assignments'."

"What do you think is happening?"

"The only thing I know is that the Akota leadership has removed all Humani and any Akota senior officer that would claim loyalty to Stone from the fight against the Xen." He paused. "All except the one that *should* be by his side."

"They want you all in one place?"

"And they want us busy," replied Vae. "No...occupied."

***

"Well, so far so good," said Orion as she turned toward Stone. "We used platinum-based stocks from the Delta system for payment. Figured it was safer than Humani or Akota currency."

"Good idea," replied Stone. "Wolf team, *Hydra*," he spoke into his comms link, "report status."

"Beacon dropped," came Katalya's reply. "We're standing by."

Stone looked toward his watch: 1:50. Like Orion said, so far things had gone well. The docking was easy; they had paid for undocumented docking and access and they had been left alone. The message burst was sent and Crow's fleet was on the way. It was almost time. "I'll head back to the others."

"Better buckle up," warned Orion. "In eight minutes you're in for the ride of your life."

"Just get us there in one piece," replied Stone.

"No promises…this is strictly point and shoot."

With a nod, Stone turned and made his way back to the others.

"Seven minutes!" he heard Martin shout as he entered the troop compartment before she sat into her chair and strapped in. "Glad you could join us, sir," she said with a smile as she tied her scarlet hair into a pony-tail. After she finished, she took a deep breath and exhaled before turning back to him. "You ready?"

"Just like old times," he replied.

"Just remember," she said, her smile fading. "You're not a Marshal today…today you're a warrior."

***

"Where is Councilman Coppertee?" asked Sierra.

"He has arrived on Port Royal, Commander," replied Councilwoman Woodstock. "He should be here shortly."

Sierra's throat vibrated with a low growl. The other Council members had gathered in the Hall and were anxiously awaiting the revelation of the threat.

All but Coppertree.

Sierra could kill the twelve that were here and then go after Coppertree but killing all of them at once would be much tidier. She activated her comms link. "Sergeant Hale, have you met with Councilmen Coppertree?"

'Yes, Commander,' came the reply. "He has just disembarked and we are on the way with him and one security guard."

"Very well," she replied. One guard—she had sent three of her warriors in case the Councilman had full contingent. "Ensure he gets here quickly…the others are waiting."

"Aye, Commander."

"He should be here in a few moments…" Sierra said to Woodstock. She looked around the room. Each council member was accompanied by two or three guards and their administrative aide. Then she scanned the edges of the Hall.

Two dozen of her men lined the walls. It would be over in seconds. "...then you'll know the nature of the threat," she added.

***

Dan-Lee took stock of the Humani guards escorting him and Councilman Coppertree to the Hall. He had known something was wrong as soon as Coppertree had been recalled, but the warriors confirmed it. The way they carried themselves, their weaponry...all of it reminded him of the Elite Guard. But they were different.

"Sergeant," asked Dan-Lee, "why isn't the Elite Guard performing this duty?"

The sergeant turned toward Dan-Lee. "Because none of your fucking business, guard." He stopped and stepped in close to Dan-Lee. "Just keep your mouth shut and follow us."

"Sorry," replied Dan-Lee, feigning fear. "I didn't mean to ruffle your feathers."

The sergeant turned away.

"I mean..." continued Dan-Lee, "I just don't know why the ProConsul would send assassins to be security guards."

The sergeant spun around. "What did—"

Dan-Lee's pistol was against the sergeant's forehead in a flash. The crack of his pistol was still echoing through the landing platform as he turned and fired into the chest of the second Humani. He swung his pistol toward the last warrior but tumbled backwards as the warrior slammed into him.

Dan-Lee hit the ground and brought his hand upward to press against the warrior as his opponent lunged toward his neck, teeth snapping. Pushing hard against the jaw of the warrior, he reached for the second pistol in his vest and shoved it in his opponent's gut. He squeezed the trigger and felt the warrior's body convulse.

But the warrior did not relent.

"What the—"

He fired again. And again.

With the third shot, the warrior's body when limp and Dan-Lee shoved him clear.

Dan-Lee jumped to his feet. He sensed movement and spun to his right as the second warrior leapt toward him from two meters away. He fired just as it reached him.

The round tore through the warrior's head, causing his body to bend backwards mid-air and fall to the ground.

"Fucking die," cursed Dan-Lee as he fired another round into the warrior.

The third warrior was slowly pushing himself off the ground.

"What are you?" asked Dan-Lee, his weapon leveled at the wounded man.

"We are the will of the ProConsul," grumbled the warrior as it reached for its comms link. "And we—"

Dan-Lee's pistol recoiled again and the warriors head snapped to the left.

"Son of a bitch," huffed Dan-Lee as he again scanned the area. "There you are," he said as he saw Councilman Coppertree, his body pressed against the wall, shaking with terror.

"What the hell was that?" gasped Coppertree. "Why did you do that?"

"They were going to kill you. And by default me," replied Dan-Lee. "I'd hoped they were actually part of a protective detail and I could use them to find a way to get to Alpha Humana but that's apparently not going to happen."

"What do you mean? What are you talking about?"

"I've been waiting a long time to get my revenge against the Ragna family and I thought the Association might lead to a chance at getting on Alpha Humana. But that's all fucked now. I'm guessing the rest of the Council is dead or soon will be."

"Dead? But why?"

"I'm guessing the Humani have grown tired of your duplicity…or just decided to cut out their middle man in the Dark Zone."

"What are we going to do now?"

"Well, we're getting off this moon." He grabbed Coppertree by the collar. "And you're staying with me until I figure out if I can still use you."

***

Orion looked at her watch. 1:58

"Here goes nothing," she said aloud as she activated *Hydra II*'s thrusters and detached from the mooring locks.

'Vessel 1862, this is Port Royal docking control. We have detected thruster activity and detachment from moorings.'

"Yes, control. We are detaching for a test of our stabilizing unit."

'Thruster testing should be preceded with a 20 minute notification, Vessel 1862.'

"Sorry," replied Orion. "We'll just be a second." She deselected the comms bridge to the control station and depressed the combat mode selector on the control panel. "Shit's about to get real."

Orion watched as the status display updated as *Hydra II* morphed into its combat configuration. She activated the combat data suite and weapons status and tracking displays appeared on a screen above her. "There we go, baby," said Orion, as the tracking screen flashed green as four large ships appeared on the display. A second later her screen identified the ships as Terillian battleships. "Here we go." She activated

144

the NAVSYS and punched in the orders Rickover had provided.

'Vessel 1862 what is—standby...'

"They must have picked up the battleships," she said, activating the ship's intercom. "Everyone hold on!" she ordered.

'All vessels, this is Port Royal control. All vessels standby for mooring lockdown. Emergency defense measures are being activated. All vessels are directed to maintain all crewmembers onboard.'

"Standby for jump in 3...2...1..."

***

Councilwoman Woodstock looked up from the panel at her chair. "The Terillians are attacking!"

"What?" asked Sierra.

"Four Akota battleships just jumped into orbit and have opened fire on our outer defenses."

"Damn it," she cursed.

"Is that the threat? Why did you wait to tell us?" pleaded Woodstock.

"Sergeant Hale, report location," said Sierra, ignoring Woodstock. "Sergeant Hale."

ALL SECURITY PERSONNEL REPORT TO YOUR STATIONS. MAN ALL AIR DEFENSE STATIONS. LAUNCH ALL AIRCRAFT.

"What is happening?" asked Woodstock again as she rose from her chair.

Sierra looked around the room. It had went to shit but her mission was still clear.

"All Dog Soldiers, this is Commander Skye. Commence Operation Black. Commence Operation Black."

Woodstock turned toward Sierra. "What is operat—"

Sierra snatched a sword from her back with one hand as she drew her pistol with the other. Sweeping downward, she slashed through the chest of one guard and the abdomen of a second in one motion as she fired her pistol into the forehead of Woodstock's third guard. As the guards fell to the ground, she sent two rounds into the chest of Woodstock's aide.

"No!" screamed Woodstock as gunfire and screams filled the Hall. She collapsed to her knees.

"The ProConsul sends her regards," said Sierra with a smile as she pressed the barrel of her pistol to the top of Woodstock's head and fired.

Sierra holstered her pistol as she looked around the Hall. Her men had been quick and efficient. Twelve councilmen, their guards, and their aides were dead. But what were the Terillians doing here so soon. She paced back and forth in thought. 'And why only four battleships?' she pondered. "Shit," she said, stopping in her tracks. "It's a diversion."

"Commander?" asked a nearby lieutenant.

"The Akota, Lieutenant Denton…they are coming for the council too." She activated her comms link. "Lieutenant Toliver, send spin message to the ProConsul and the Doran fleet. Inform them the operation is underway and that 12 of 13 Council members are dead. Thirteenth is unaccounted for. Additionally, four Akota battleships have begun bombardment of Port Royal defenses. Recommend Doran fleet jump immediately."

'Aye, Commander,' came the reply from her communications officer.

Sierra slid her sword into its sheath and gripped her assault rifle. "Lieutenant Denton, position your men on the exterior of the building but stay hidden until I give you the order to fire. Lieutenant Kawal," she continued, "disperse our men in defensive positions throughout the Hall…Scout Rangers will be arriving soon."

Sierra's heart rate increased. Stone and Martin would be coming too.

***

Orion forced air form her lungs. "Shit," she cursed, struggling to stay conscious. The jump from the dock to the security had occurred in the blink of eye but she felt as if her insides were still at the docking station as she let out a deep grunt. Her eyes began to focus and she saw the security gate in front of her. She took manual control of the plasma cannons and directed them toward the barrier.

"Katalya, Magnus, get your heads down," she warned as she pulled the trigger.

The security gate evaporated in a ball of fire.

"Landing," she said into the communicator as she lowered the ship to the surface.

'On the way,' came Magnus' voice in reply.

"Roger. Port doors open."

Orion scanned the exterior viewing panels and looked through the cockpit. The plasma cannons had done the trick, no defenders were left to return fire.

'Onboard,' reported Katalya.

"Roger," answered Orion. "Buckle up!"

Orion pushed *Hydra II* through the massive hole in the barrier created by the cannons. Once on the other side, she punched in new coordinates in NAVSYS for the Council Hall. She took another deep breath, still not fully recovered from the last jump. "Shit." She activated the intercom. "Jumping in 3...2...1..."

***

Stone's stomach clinched tight and his muscles convulsed as his vision blurred. Shaking his head, he focused on a single point on the deck to gain his bearings.

"Fuck," huffed Martin. "That sucked."

"Good luck!" came Orion's voice over the intercom as the lights above the door shifted to green and hatches dropped open.

"Go!" shouted Stone as he unlatched his harness and leapt through the hatch.

He hit the ground with Martin and Crowdog in front of him. Martin had taken cover next to a brick wall and Crowdog was moving forward to find a position to cover them.

Stone rushed to the wall and fell into position beside Martin. He felt Shara take up position beside him.

"Alpha team's out," reported Martin.

'Roger,' came Orion's voice over the comms circuit. 'Lifting off to drop Bravo.'

Stone turned his head to the left away from the dust and debris filling the air as *Hydra II* lifted off.

"Where are their defenses?" asked Stone.

"I don't know," replied Martin. "But we need to move up."

Stone felt a knot in his stomach. "Something's not right."

"I know," said Martin. "But we can't stay here."

"Go," ordered Stone.

"Moving," replied Martin before she leapt over the wall toward the entrance to the Hall.

As Stone and the others ran toward the entrance, the lack of gunfire was unnerving. Even if the Association had been taken by surprise, there should be a few guards trying to stop them. In a few seconds they reached the Hall and stacked up next to the door.

"Something's fucky about this," Martin said to Stone.

"We should have taken some fire already," added Shara.

Stone could see the concern on Martin's face. He nodded.

"Crowdog, report status," she ordered into the comms link.

No reply.

'Bravo on the deck,' came over their circuits.

"Crowdog, report," Martin repeated, this time in Akota. She turned toward Stone and shook her head. "This is—"

The thud of bodies hitting the ground stopped Martin mid-sentence.

"Damn it," cursed Stone as he saw Crowdog and another man lying on the ground next to him. Crowdog had a huge gash across his chest but his sword was protruding from the side of the man's body. The other man jerked up from the ground, the blade still embedded in his body.

Martin's rifled barked and a salvo knocked the man back to the ground.

"Look at his neck," said Shara. "The Akota."

Crowdog's neck looked like an animal had torn a chunk out of it.

"It's like one of the Wolf Clan had taken a bite out of his neck," said Martin.

Stone shifted his rifle and scanned the walkways above them. "Check the other body," he ordered as he kept watch for movement above them.

Martin knelt next to the man lying next to Crowdog. Placing her hand near the man's mouth she pushed his mouth open. "Fucking fangs," she declared.

"It must be the other group they were testing on Venato," said Stone. His teeth gnashed in his mouth. "Everyone be advised," he ordered into the comms link, "modified soldiers are in play."

"Sir," said Martin, gaining his attention. "Charges are placed...are we going."

He exhaled hard. "Go!"

"Breaching!" yelled Shara and a series of charges around the door exploded, sending a shock wave that rattled Stone's bones.

Martin spun into the entrance but instantly fell backward and curled into a ball as an explosion of gunfire erupted sending lead flying through the opening.

***

As the rattle of gunfire echoed in the distance, Katalya threw herself over the ledge onto the walkway above the Hall.

Her feet hit the ground and her nostril's instantly flared, taking in a powerful scent. Her hair bristled and she felt her canines extend in her mouth. "No," she snarled as she activated her comms. "Magnus...they are here...the Xen dogs."

"I can smell them too," came his reply.

Katalya lifted her head in the air and inhaled, closing her eyes. He eyes popped open and she spun around just as someone slammed into her. The two tumbled to the walkway, Katalya's heart pounding and a rage born of instinct coursing through her body. Letting out a growl, she rolled on top of her attacker.

The man looked up with his mouth open and teeth dripping with saliva.

He lunged upward, snapping at Katalya's face but she landed a fist against his temple. His head bounced off the walkway and Katalya shoved it back onto the metallic grating, pinning him. She let out a howl and sank her teeth into the man's neck. She bit down hard and then twisted her head upward, tearing a chunk of the man's flesh from his body. "Fucking Xen animals," she cursed as she spat meat from her mouth. Katalya grabbed her rifle and leveled it on two more attackers rushing toward her. Her rifle recoiled as she sent a burst into the attackers. She moved forward and fired another burst into the chest of one of the men when he tried to rise from the walkway. At the bodies, she placed the barrel of her rifle against the forehead of the first man and fired. Then the second.

She sniffed the air. "Walkway is clear," she reported.

***

"Bravo team is inside," reported Thay.

"Roger," replied Orion through the comms link. "Headed to the west side to provide cover for Alpha."

"Moving into the Hall," Thay replied as his team began to move forward. In a few meters, they reached the corner. Thay held his rifle to his shoulder and pivoted into the passageway. As he did, his sights fell on two enemy soldiers facing the opposite direction.

Thay slowly lowered his rifle and drew his tomahawks.

Letting out a grunt, Thay hurled the tomahawk in his right hand toward one of the soldiers and quickly shifted his body, sending the second flying toward the other. The first tomahawk sank into the back of the soldier's skull, his body crumpling to the ground.

Just as the second tomahawk was about the hit the remaining soldier, he spun around, curving his body backwards as the blade passed over his body.

Thay grabbed his rifle and swung it toward the soldier but Littledove had already reacted. The Akota leapt forward into a roll, drawing his sword as he did. Rising to his feet just as the enemy soldier regained his balance, Littledove drove his sword into the soldier's gut.

The enemy soldier let out a growl and landed a hard right hand against Littledove's jaw sending him to his knees. The soldier, with Littledove's sword protruding from his torso, leveled his pistol toward the Scout Ranger.

Before he could pull the trigger, Magnus slammed into his body. Driving the soldier against the wall, Magnus wrenched his enemies hand away from his body. He let out a growl and lunged for the soldier's neck. He bit down hard but released with a howl of pain as the soldier drove a knife into his thigh.

As Magnus stumbled backwards, Thay pulled the tomahawk from the wall. He pivoted and drove the tomahawk into his opponent's neck, nearly decapitating him.

"Damn it," cursed Littledove as he pulled his sword from the soldier's body. "He wouldn't fucking die."

"Most will be like that," grumbled Magnus as he pulled the knife from his thigh. "Instinct—and rage—will take over." He paused to apply coagulate gel to his leg. "Treat them like rabid dogs."

"Rabid dogs with automatic rifles," added Littledove.

"They bleed, so they will die," said Thay. "We need to keep moving."

Chapter 9

Stone exhaled heavily, his back pressed against the exterior wall of the Council Hall as bullets whizzed past him.

He looked at his watch. "Damn it," he cursed as he looked up to Martin who was leaning against the opposite side of the entrance. "Get Orion."

"Roger," replied Martin, activating her link. "Orion, get your ass over to this side," she ordered as bullets ricocheted off the brick wall behind her. She pivoted and fired a burst into the entrance to the Hall. "We need—" She swung her rifle toward the walkway above her and fired. "Shara, the walkway," she ordered as an enemy soldier fell to the ground. She activated the comms link again. "We can't make entry. We need your guns."

'On the way,' came Orion's reply.

"I'm in route too," added Katalya. "'My team is in."

Martin looked toward Stone. "We've got to get in there; our timeline's already fucked."

'Get clear and get your head's down,' came Orion's voice.

"Back over the wall!" ordered Stone, pushing himself from the exterior wall and leaping over the brick wall a few meters from the main building.

Hitting the ground with a grunt, he looked up to see Martin and Shara on his side of the wall. "We're—"

Stone's voice was cut short as the gatling guns from *Hydra II* erupted.

Stone curled his body as the heavy baritone *brrrrrt* of the guns drowned out everything. He looked up to see his companions doing the same as debris landed all around them.

After a few seconds, the rumble of the guns shifted to a high whine as the rotary guns began to spin down after Orion stopped firing.

'Door's open,' reported Orion. 'Really open.'

Stone peered over the wall.

Where the entrance to the Hall had been, there was now a hole large enough to drive a main hover tank through. Bodies of Humani were strewn through the debris.

'You're welcome,' said Orion.

Stone saw Katalya leap from the elevated walkway onto the ground.

"They'll all modified. The Dog Soldiers from the Venato."

"How many?" asked Stone, his stomach tightening.

"A lot."

Stone exhaled heavily. "Let's go!" ordered Stone. "We've got some time to make up."

***

On the other end of the building, Thay, Magnus, and Littledove moved quickly through the passageway toward the center of the Hall. Thay shifted his rifle from left to center, then right as the group crept toward the end of the passageway. As he reached the end, he saw a stairwell. "I'll cover up," he said to the others. "You two move to the first floor."

Magnus and Littledove acknowledged with a nod.

Thay stepped into the vestibule and Magnus and Littledove rushed past him to the next level. He saw a flash of movement and fired.

A soldier fell from the platform above, landing at Thay's feet as he centered his rifle on another rushing down the stairway and fired. "Go!" he shouted to Magnus and Littledove, noticing they had paused halfway down the stairway to the first floor. "I'll cover you!" Thay shifted his body and fired again as another soldier leaned over the ledge above and fired. His aim was true and the man fell backwards out of sight. Another soldier leapt from the platform above. Thay swung his rifle toward the threat but the soldier crashed into him, knocking him to the ground.

The soldier pressed down on Thay's chest, his fangs flashing bright as he drove his head toward Thay's neck. Thay shoved his hand against the neck of his attacker and pushed the snapping jaws clear. As the enemy's head shifted to his left, Thay wrapped his left arm around the soldier and quickly locked in his choke hold with his right, squeezing hard.

Thay felt his body lifted off the ground as the soldier swung his body forward into a squat and pushed upward. In response, he wrapped his legs around the attacker's torso and arched his back to prevent his opponent from flipping him into the air.

Thay tightened his body, letting out a grunt as the soldier slammed him into the wall. Recovering from the impact, he released his right hand and grabbed a knife from his vest. In doing so, his hold weakened and his opponent pulled his head from Thay's grip.

Pain shot through Thay's shoulder as the soldier sank its teeth into his flesh but he remained focused, driving his blade into his opponent's back.

The soldier released his bite and stumbled backwards.

Thay pulled a tomahawk from his belt and lunged forward but quickly dropped to his knees and arched his back as the soldier slashed at him with a sword. The air from the blade washed over the bare skin on his scalp just before he pushed his torso erect and drove the blade of his tomahawk into the soldier's thigh. Thay's opponent let out a howl and brought the handle of his sword down against Thay's temple. Dazed, Thay swung his pistol upward as the soldier raised his hands above his head.

Thay fired three rounds into the man's chest, knocking him to the ground.

Rising to his feet, he looked down the barrel at the man's head and fired a final shot.

Grimacing from the pain now radiating down his left arm, he reached down and picked up his rifle with his right. Trying to ignore the pain, he rushed down the stairs to catch up to Magnus and Littledove.

At the bottom of the stairs Thay heard the sounds of a struggle and brought his rifle to the ready. Stepping into a large oval room he saw Magnus falling backwards as Littledove lunged toward a female officer with shoulder-length black hair.

The officer blocked Littledove's thrust with the sword in her left hand and slammed the handle of the sword in her right into his temple.

Thay centered his sights on the officer but just as he was about to pull the trigger, Magnus flashed into his view as he crashed into the officer. "Damn it," cursed Thay as he let his rifle fall to the side and grabbed a tomahawk with each hand and rushed toward the melee.

The officer hit the floor face-first but swung her elbow upward, connecting with Magnus' jaw. As he recoiled, she flipped onto her back and grabbed the sword that had been jarred from her left hand. Magnus rolled backwards from atop her as the officer slashed at his torso.

Magnus leapt to his feet but stumbled.

Blood began to seep through his torn vest as Littledove and Thay converged on the officer.

A sword in each hand, the officer stepped back, blocking Thay's tomahawk as he slashed at her chest and driving her boot into Littledove's knee as he thrust with his sword. Littledove dropped to one knee and the officer leapt over him pivoting mid-air. As she landed she drove the sword in her right hand through Littledove's back.

The Akota warrior let out a groan and arched his back as the sword exploded through his chest. The enemy officer raised her other sword above her head but as she swung downward a round from Magnus' pistol tore into her thigh.

Falling to her knees, she let out a deep growl and drove the other sword into Littledove's back. She drew her pistol from it holster as she rolled to her right away from Magnus. Magnus' next shots missed and she turned back toward him from the ground and fired two shots into his abdomen.

Thay dropped his tomahawk and grabbed his rifle, bringing it to his shoulder.

Hot, burning pain raced through his arm as a round from the officer's pistol bore into his arm just below the wound the other Dog Soldier had given him.

He raised his rifle again.

"Ah-ah," said the officer as she held her pistol on Thay.

She drew another pistol from her vest, holding it on Magnus as he struggled to push himself up from the floor. "You too...brother," she spat.

Thay stared defiantly into her green eyes, panting as he tried to push the pain from his consciousness. He watched as she walked back to the body of Littledove. He was on his knees, leaning forward with two swords protruding through his chest, holding him off the floor.

"Drop the rifle," she ordered. "Let's finish this like warriors. Your tomahawks and its fangs," she added without looking at Magnus, "against my swords and fangs."

Despite the pain in his arm, a smile came to Thay's face as he unclipped the lanyard from his rifle and let it fall to the ground. "So be it." He drew his tomahawk.

"Good," she replied as she holstered her pistols and yanked the swords from Littledove's corpse. "If you tell me where the traitors Stone and Martin are, I promise to kill you quickly," she added before turning toward Magnus. "You...animal...will die slowly if I have my way."

"Then let us see if you can," grumbled Magnus as he pulled the damaged vest off his body and dropped his combat belt.

Thay stepped toward her.

"No!" grunted Magnus. "She is mine."

Thay feared Magnus was too injured but nodded in acknowledgement.

"Cute," said the officer as she sheathed her swords. "Let's get primal," she growled as she showed her fangs.

Magnus rushed toward the officer but she closed the ground quickly and leapt into the air as the two collided. She latched onto Magnus torso and neck and spun her body behind his, wrapping her legs around his neck and twisting his body to the ground. He was rising when she slammed her fist into his face, knocking him to the ground again. She pinned his head to the floor with one hand and grabbed his left arm and slammed it to the floor.

Magnus eyes opened wide as his nostrils flared. "You're her—"

"No!" shouted Thay as he rushed toward Magnus.

But he was too late.

Sierra opened her mouth wide and sank her teeth into Magnus' neck. He let out a howl as she jerked her head upward violently, sending blood and flesh flying from Magnus' body.

Sierra spun around and jumped to her feet to face Thay.

Thay stopped a few meters away from her. Her lower jaw was covered in Magnus' blood as it dripped onto her uniform.

"Guess I had to settle for killing it quick," said Sierra, her mouth still full of flesh and blood.

"What are you?" asked Thay.

"I'm the ProConsul's angel of death, you Terillian trash."

"The ProConsul seems to have a lot of those," replied Thay as he heard muffled gunfire from somewhere in the building. "One of her former 'angels' will be here soon."

Sierra glanced toward the far entrance as a smile came to her face. "Martin?"

"But don't worry about her," replied Thay. "Because I am going to take your life before she gets here."

Sierra pulled her swords from their sheaths. "Then come take it," she said with a blood-soaked smile.

Thay rushed forward as the officer readied herself.

Feigning a strike with his tomahawk, Thay dropped to the ground and slammed his boot into Sierra's injured leg.

She dropped to one knee but drove the sword in her right hand toward Thay's torso. He directed the sword away from his body with his tomahawk but when he tried to push himself up, his injured left arm failed him and he rolled away to make space between him and his opponent.

Thay pushed himself to his knees and swung downward with his tomahawk, driving the slashing sword of Sierra to floor. As the metallic clang of the tomahawk's blade sliding off the sword echoed across the room, he exploded from his position and slammed into Sierra's torso, lifting her into the air. Thay grunted through the pain as she slammed the handle of her sword into his injured shoulder and pivoted to slam her onto the floor. He heard the air leave her lungs and rose up to his knees, cocking his tomahawk above his head.

A powerful blow to his exposed side caused him to pause and a second caused him to curl his body to his right. He raised his tomahawk again but his body spasmed and his weapon fell to the floor as the searing pain of a blade sliding into his left side shot through his body. He let out a gasp as his left lung collapsed.

Another blow to Thay's jaw knocked him off the officer and he fell onto his back, still trying to bring in enough air. Looking up he saw the officer standing above him.

"You're not bad, Terillian," she said as Thay felt the tip of a sword press against his chest. "Too bad you were already injured."

"Wh—who…are…you?" he huffed, slowly wrapping his hand around the tomahawk lying beside him.

"I am Commander Sierra Skye," she said.

He gasped again as she slowly sank the sword into his abdomen.

"Where are they?" she asked. "Tell me and I will end it quickly."

Thay let out a raspy groan as the sword sank deeper into his body.

He looked up toward her.

"Where? I promise—"

Thay jerked the tomahawk off the floor and drove the spiked end into the officer's foot.

A howl escaped the officer as she drove the sword deep into his abdomen.

Gasping for air, Thay pulled a pistol from his vest and swung it toward the officer but stopped as his eyes focused on the barrel of rifle pointed at his head.

"Enough!" grumbled the officer. "Time to say hello to your ancestors."

Thay shifted his gaze to the deep green eyes of his opponent. "So be it."

Sierra lowered her head to line up her shot.

Thay's eyes were still focused on his opponent's when her attention shifted and she spun to her right just as a bullet slammed into her shoulder.

***

"Damn it," cursed Martin as she saw Sierra disappear from her sights. "She moved at the last minute...winged her."

"Thay, come in," ordered Stone into the comms circuit as he stood next to Martin at the opposite entrance to the hall.

"Magnus? Littledove?" He looked toward Martin and shook his head.

"Magnus!" shouted Katalya across the hall. "Magnus!"

Stone could see Katalya's eyes were screaming with anxiety. He looked across the large hall. Thay was at best severely injured on the other side. He exhaled heavily. "Shara, you cover the right. Katalya...Katalya!" shouted Stone to get her attention.

He saw the look in her eyes.

"No!" he Stone as Katalya rushed forward. "Shit," he cursed as he swung his rifle back toward the hall. "Everyone move up."

Stone shifted his rifle from left to right and then back as he moved forward. "Katalya, stop!" he yelled across the hall to no avail.

Moving across the floor, Stone suddenly stopped. "No," he huffed, dropping to one knee.

He had found Thay.

"Thay," he said as he pressed his hand over blood oozing from the warrior's stomach. After another quick scan of the area, he looked over Thay's body. Aside from the wound to his abdomen, Thay's shoulder was mangled and his left sleeve was soaked in blood. "Thay."

Thay slowed opened his eyes and coughed, spitting up blood. "She was…fast…" He coughed again. "…and st—strong."

That officer?" asked Stone.

"S—she did this…to all…of us."

"What?"

"Green eyes," said Thay, almost whispering before fading into unconsciousness.

"It's okay, brother," said Stone, turning toward Shara. "He needs meds."

"Got it, sir," replied Shara as he knelt next to Stone. "We'll have you fixed up in no time," he said as he injected a neuro-med into Thay's thigh.

Stone again scanned the room. "Where are the others?"

"The Akota captain's over here," answered Martin from a few meters away. "Dead," she added as she held her rifle in the direction of a nearby stairway.

Stone's jaw tightened. "Where's—"

A scream echoed across the hall, sending a jolt down Stone's spine.

Katalya had found Magnus.

"No!" cried out Katalya as she collapsed onto the body of Magnus. "No!" she wailed again, throwing her head toward the ceiling.

"Damn it," cursed Stone as he jumped to his feet and rushed to her.

His heart sank when he reached her. She was on her knees, holding the bloody body of Magnus in her arms.

"Katalya…"

"He's dead," she panted, running her hand over Magnus' forehead.

Stone had no answer for her pain.

He knelt next to her.

Martin, still scanning the room, backed away from the stairway and next to Stone and Katalya. She looked to Shara as he applied coagulate to Thay's injuries.

"Even with the meds, we need to get him to a doc fast…he's pretty messed up," said Shara.

Stone looked away from Magnus to Thay, and then toward Littledove. "One soldier did this."

"What?" asked Martin. Her face grew red and her jaw clinched. She looked back toward the stairway. "Where the fuck is she?"

"Ground teams," came Orion's voice over the circuit. "Fleet comms just lit up. They're picking up multiple neutrino spikes…a report of Doran ships just came across the fleet tactical circuit."

"Doran?" replied Stone.

"What the fuck are they doing here?" asked Martin.

Martin's concern was warranted. Stone took in the scene around him. Association security guards and what looked like most of the Council members lay dead all around them. Among the dead were some Humani Dog soldiers. He glanced toward Littledove's body and then toward Shara as he worked to stop Thay's bleeding. Then he looked down at Magnus, still resting in Katalya's arms.

"Orion, pick us up at the east end...now."

'Roger,' replied Orion. 'I'll be waiting on you.'

"What about that officer?" asked Martin. "We need to go after her."

"We don't leave until she's dead," added Katalya, looking up from Magnus' body.

"Katalya," said Stone. "We have to get Thay to one of our ships and—"

"Then you take him," interrupted Katalya, her face red and her cheeks wet with tears.

'On station,' reported Orion. 'You need to hurry...we have confirmation of Doran fleet in orbit—battlecruisers and orbital destroyers. Admiral Crow he's outnumbered and will jump soon.'

"Shit. How long?" asked Stone.

'Five minutes.'

Stone looked toward Martin. He could see her body was tight, the thought of fighting the woman who had taken out the others consuming her. "We go now," said Stone. "If we don't go now, we might not get out."

"I don't care," replied Katalya as she stood over Magnus' body.

"I'll stay with her," added Martin. "That bitch needs to pay."

Stone locked his gaze on Martin, hoping his stare would be enough.

Martin let out an audible groan. "Yes, sir."

"Shara, Martin, grab Thay," ordered Stone.

'Doran dropships inbound.' reported Orion. "Where are you?"

"On the way," replied Stone, turning toward Katalya.

"No!" shouted Katalya. "I'm not...I can't."

Stone looked toward Martin again.

Martin nodded and walked to Katalya.

"Don't try to stop me," grunted Katalya, her fangs showing.

Martin partially raised her hands in the air. "I know it hurts."

"Do you?" snapped Katalya. "Do you know what it's like to lose everything?"

Martin stepped in close to Katalya.

"Emily?" said Stone softly, unsure of her next move.

Martin placed her hands on Katalya's shoulders. "I do…and I promise you she will die." Martin moved her right hand to Katalya's cheek. "But not today."

Martin caught Katalya as she collapsed into her arms.

"I promise," said Martin quietly into Katalya's ear. "But we have to stay alive to take our revenge," she added as she helped Katalya regain her balance.

Katalya replied with a weak nod of concession.

'Where the fuck are you guys?' blared Orion's voice over the comms circuit.

"On the way," replied Stone. He let his rifle fall to his side and knelt to pick up Magnus' body.

"Leave him," said Katalya. "I don't need his body because I know I had his heart."

With a nod, Stone rose. "Ready?"

"Ready," replied Shara as he hefted the unconscious Thay over his shoulder.

"Ready," added Katalya weakly.

With Stone in the lead, they made their way to the exit.

"We're coming out," reported Stone.

'Hurry up,' answered Orion.

Stone opened the door and stepped outside. *Hydra II* was in a hover a meter off the ground 100 meters away. He scanned the area as Shara moved past him, carrying Thay.

Martin followed. As they passed, he turned back toward Katalya and grabbed her arm. "Let's go."

'Incoming dropships,' warned Orion.

Stone looked upward as two dropships slammed onto the ground.

"Go!" he shouted as he and Katalya began to sprint toward *Hydra II*. As they ran toward *Hydra II*, Stone heard the sound of the first dropship's troop doors slamming open. Stone leveled his weapon toward the open hatch and—

The rattle of *Hydra II's* guns roared over the hum of the dropships' engines as her rounds ripped through the first Doran ship, sending metal and flesh flying through the open hatch.

Stone shifted his aim toward the second ship.

Two tall figures emerged from the dropship. They wore light but visible power armor and their heads were covered with armored helmets and visors illuminated with a blue hue.

Stone centered his sights and fired a burst from his rifle.

The rounds hit the first soldier, causing him to stumble but not fall.

"Damn it," cursed Stone and he took aim again and sent a run into the center of the soldier's helmet. He heard the metallic clang as the bullet tore through the helmet, toppling the soldier.

173

He shifted his fire but rounds from Martin, Shara, and Katalya peppered the second soldier.

More soldiers began to emerge as the four poured rounds into the hatch.

Stone pressed the release for his magazine and was inserting another when he saw Martin flash into his view near the dropship's hatch. As she reached the ship, another solider emerged and Martin slashed at his chest with her sword.

The Doran soldier raised its arm and Martin's sword glanced off the armor before he delivered a blow that sent Martin tumbling backwards.

Martin rolled to her right and jumped to her feet just as rounds from Shara's rifle staggered the Doran.

The Doran turned toward Shara but when it did, Martin stepped in and drove her sword into the soldier's side just under the body armor. She ripped the sword back out, pivoted her torso, and drove the sword into the soldier's neck just below his helmet. As the Doran fell, Martin pulled a grenade from her vest and tossed it into the open hatch.

A damped explosion sent smoke and debris flying from the hatch as Martin and Shara rushed back toward Thay. Just as they reached the unconscious warrior, Stone saw motion at the hatch of the first dropship and brought his weapon to bear as a massive robotic war machine stomped out of the dropship. After exiting, the mech extended its four legs as two compartments opened on its armored body, allowing two large caliber guns to present themselves. The mech, close to three meters tall, spun its guns toward Stone and Katalya.

"Move!" shouted Stone as he dove to his right just at the mech's big guns opened fire.

Stone rose to his knees and opened fire. His shots, and those of the others, ricocheted of the mech's body. He saw the guns turn toward Martin and Shara with a metallic hum. "Get down—"

The mech exploded in a ball of fire as *Hydra II*'s plasma cannons found their target.

"Thanks," said Stone into his comms link.

'Just quick fuckin' around get on the fucking ship,' came Orion's reply.

Stone and Katalya covered Martin and Stone as they carried Thay onto *Hydra II* then followed them onboard.

Just as Stone reached the hatch, he looked back to see several more dropships in the distance.

The days of Port Royal's duplicity were over.

Once onboard, Stone's attention turned to Thay. He stood over Martin and Shara as they checked the still unconscious warrior.

"We've done all we can do," said Shara.

"How is he?" asked Stone.

"Alive…" replied Martin. "But we need to get him onboard one of the orbital destroyers fast."

Stone activated the intercom on the bulkhead. "We're onboard. Let's get out of here."

'We're gone,' replied Orion.

Stone grabbed a nearby stanchion to balance himself as *Hydra II* rose from the ground and banked hard and accelerated toward the upper atmosphere.

"What the fuck was all of that?" asked Martin. "Doran dropships, that mech…and there's no way one person took out two painted faces and Magnus."

"All those Humani soldiers…they were like Magnus and Katalya," replied Stone, "but with Guard-style training."

"They are not like us," said Katalya, looking up from her seated position, her face red with anger. "They're animals, loyal to the Xen and genetically driven to hate."

"You don't need biology to hate," replied Martin. "You just need a reason," she added as she walked to Katalya and placed her hand on Katalya's shoulder. "Before this is over, all of them…the Xen, the First Families, Astra Varus…and her pets will pay for all of the evil they have done."

'Everyone buckle up,' ordered Orion over the intercom. "Admiral Crow just passed coordinates. He's lost one of the destroyers and he's jumping now."

"Will he make it?" asked Stone, looking toward Thay.

"I don't know, sir," replied Shara.

"Ask Crow to wait two more minutes," said Stone into the intercom. "We need to get Thay to the docs."

"They've already jumped," replied Orion.

"Damn it," cursed Stone. Hopefully the jump isn't a long one.

Stone rushed toward the cockpit, stepping through just as *Hydra II* exited Port Royal's atmosphere. Looking back he saw blotches of the surface darkening. "What's that?"

"The Dorans probably took out some of the atmospheric control stations or damaged some of the transit ports that help maintain the habitat," replied Orion. "There's probably thousands dying from scattered loss of atmospheric control across the city. If—" She stopped mid-sentence.

"What is it?"

"Look," replied Orion, pointing toward the cockpit window.

Dozens of Doran capital ships floated in orbit with hundreds of fighters and dropships headed toward the moon.

"Strap in," continued Orion as she ran her finger over the navigation panel, dragging the jump coordinates provided by Admiral Crow to *Hydra II's* jump computer input. "It should be a short jump."

Stone's attention was drawn to a red flashing light on the ship's self-defense panel.

"What's that?"

"Doran fighters just picked us up," replied Orion. "But don't worry…we'll be gone before they get here."

Stone saw the blue flashes outside of *Hydra II* as the jump started.

They had completed the mission, but at a heavy cost.

Chapter 10

"Commander," said Lieutenant Kawal. "Commander!"

"We need to go after them," grumbled Sierra as she pushed herself off the deck of the transport only to fall again.

"You're too badly injured, Commander," replied Kawal. "And the Dorans have started their attack."

"Where are the traitors?"

"We sent a squad back into the Council Hall after we found you but they were gone."

"How many of them did we kill?"

"The three you killed plus one more, Commander?"

"But not Stone or Martin?"

"No, Commander."

"Did we find the last Council member?"

"No, Commander. The team sent to kill him was found dead."

"Damn it," cursed Sierra, slamming her head onto the deck. "What are our casualties?"

"Five dead including Lieutenant O'Neil—"

"Shit," interrupted Sierra. "Go on."

"Five critical and ten with minor injuries. Twenty-one ready for duty."

"Do—" Sierra grunted as a wave pain washed over her. The embedded neuro-meds must have been exhausted. "Do we have a trail?"

"No, Commander," replied Kawal as he injected neuro-meds into her externally.

Sierra felt her head growing heavy almost instantly. "W— we need...need..."

"You should rest, Commander. We will get back to the frigate and start working on possible locations they could go next."

Sierra grunted, forcing herself to stay conscious. "Inform the ProConsul that all but one member of the Council has been killed." She paused, closing her eyes as she focused on her words. "And that the traitors have escaped." She opened her eyes but her vision blurred as she began to fade. "T—tell her I failed..."

Sierra's head fell back onto the deck as she lost consciousness.

***

Stone let out a sigh of relief as *Hydra II* locked into its berth onboard the orbital destroyer *Stormfall*.

"Hangar Control, *Hydra II*, on deck, requesting medical team," reported Orion.

'Roger, *Hydra II*. Medical team is en route,' came the reply.

Stone unlatched himself and rushed to the troop compartment. He arrived just as the medical team was removing Thay from ship.

"How does it look?" he asked one of the medics.

"We need to get him to medical fast, sir."

"Of course," replied Stone.

As the medical team left the ship, an Akota commander entered.

"Commander?" asked Stone.

"Marshal," replied the commander. "Admiral Crow has sent me. Just before we jumped, a small transport with Akota signatures requested to come aboard. When they docked, it was, ah…"

"What is it, Commander?"

"They asked for the female red-haired Guardsman."

"What?"

Martin's head spun toward the commander. "They asked for me?"

"Yes, Major…if you and the Marshal will come with me…he's still being held on the transport."

"Maybe it's a friend from Port Royal?" offered Orion as she entered the compartment.

"I don't have any friends," replied Martin.

"That's a good point," added Orion.

"Who would—"

"I have no idea, sir," said Martin.

Stone turned toward Orion. "Can you stay with Katalya?"

"I'll get her to her quarters," said Orion with a glance toward Katalya, who was still sitting in the troop compartment, her head in her hands.

He gave Orion a slight nod and turned back to Martin, holding out his hand toward the exit. "Lead the way, Major."

Martin and Stone made their way across the hangar to a small transport surrounded by Akota security forces.

Near the hatch stood a tall man with long blonde hair. As they grew closer, Stone noticed the man was in restraints.

"Who is that?" he asked Stone.

"No idea," replied Martin.

"Marshal Stone," said a major as he approached him and Martin. "This man came aboard using Akota military codes but clearly isn't Akota. He asked for the red-haired female Guardsman fighting with the Akota." He glanced toward Martin. "We can only assume he is referring to your Chief of Staff."

***

"Hey!" shouted Martin, stepping past the major. "Who the fuck are—"

The man turned to face Martin, stopping her in her tracks. Unlike the last time they met, hair covered his once bald head. But the eyes were unmistakable.

182

"Good to see you again, Paladin," said the man.

"No," replied Martin. "The priest?"

Stone's hand gripped his sword. "A follower of the Word?"

The man laughed. "No...that was just a role." He turned toward Martin. "It seems we all have to play roles at one time or another. Isn't that right?"

"What are you doing here?" demanded Martin.

"Easy, tiger," replied the man. "You know what I want."

"You weren't going to kill any First Family members on Port Royal," said Martin. "So no...I don't."

"Who is this?" asked Stone. "Wh—" Martin saw the flash of Stone's sword as he jerked it from its sheath. "Phelan!" he shouted as he stepped toward the man.

"Wait!" yelled Martin, stepping between Stone and the man.

"Move!" demanded Stone.

Martin saw a hatred painted on Stone's face she'd only seen a few times in the years she had known him. "Sir...wait." She placed her hand against Stone's chest. The warrior that had helped her escape and later fought her in the Echo system was the cause for Stone's reaction, but all she could think of was a blonde girl with oily hair...and a gunshot. She closed her eyes then opened them again. "Remember who we were fighting for when we went to war with the Phel." She looked into Stone's eyes. "We were nothing more than assassins for the ProConsul and First Families."

Stone's face slowly loosened. He looked past Martin toward the Phel. "Who are you and why are you here?"

"I'm Dan-Lee and I'm here because you and the Humani's little spat on Port Royal ruined the best chance I had at getting at the Ragna family, I decided my best option for getting out of here was to use what leverage I had to get clear."

"What are you talking about?" asked Stone.

"He wants to kill the family of the ProConsul that ordered the genocide of his people," said Martin, the words settling in her stomach like an anchor.

"Yes," confirmed Dan-Lee.

"Your best option?" continued Martin. "Last time I saw you, you tried to kill me…tried."

Dan-Lee smiled. "Since then, I've learned that while you…" He turned toward Stone, a scowl coming to his face. "…and this one may have been the weapons used to kill my people…" He looked back toward Martin.

Martin fought the urge to turn away, the image of that girl burned into her consciousness.

"…you were not the catalyst," continued Dan-Lee.

"How do you know what we've done?" asked Stone. "Just because we were Guardsmen—"

"Don't insult me, Marshal Stone," snapped Dan-Lee. "There are too few Phel left that all of us do not know of the man that destroyed the last real settlement on our homeland…"

Martin felt Dan-Lee's eyes squeeze her heart like a fist.

"…or the woman that nearly destroyed what was left of us."

She wanted to shake her head—tell him to stop but couldn't.

"That settlement on Golf 2 you killed so many…man, woman…"

She shook her head slightly. "No," she mouthed.

"…and child."

Martin kept her gaze locked on Dan-Lee but her eyes betrayed the pain she'd carried for years.

"Hmm," said Dan-Lee. "So maybe the Xen's pets do feel."

"If you hate us so much, then why are you here?" asked Stone.

"That's the second thing I realized. The enemy of my enemy is my friend. And since you were basically a tool used by the First Families, then I can use you too."

Martin shook her head, trying to wash the vision of the Phelian girl from her mind and focus her thoughts. "What are you talking about?"

"It appears the Association is done—torn apart between the Humani, Terillians, and the Dorans. And since the ProConsul has turned your wretched planet into a walled city, I needed to get away to find time to figure out a better plan."

"And you think you can just show up and join us?" asked Stone.

"I'm not trying to join you," laughed Dan-Lee. "I just need to get clear of the Dorans."

"So you really think it is that simple?" asked Stone.

"I do bring a few things to the table."

"Such as?"

"I have been a personal guard of Council member Coppertree for several months and have learned a lot about their operations." He paused as a smile came over his face. "And I do have a small present for you."

"What are you talking about?" asked Martin.

"Follow me," replied Dan-Lee as he turned toward the entrance to the transport.

"There's nothing in there, Marshal," reported a nearby lieutenant. "We've already swept the ship."

Martin drew her sidearm. "Did you check it for explosives?" she asked, remembering the Saint's final moments. "Did you check him for explosives?"

Dan-Lee laughed.

"He's been checked, Major," huffed the lieutenant.

"Just follow me," said Dan-Lee to Stone.

"Wait," interjected Martin. She didn't know much about Dan-Lee other than he was a great fighter and really good at being deceptive. "I'll go instead."

"Fine," replied Stone.

"Let's go, priest," said Martin as she holstered her pistol and motioned toward the transport.

"I'm no priest, Paladin," replied Dan-Lee. "Just part of the game...but again, you know about that."

"Just show me whatever you are going to show me."

Martin followed Dan-Lee into the transport, making sure to leave enough room to react if he turned on her.

"How did you know we would be here?" asked Martin as they moved through the main passageway.

"The Council members talk freely around their guards once they get comfortable with them. And they talked about you and your Marshal Stone quite a bit."

Martin swung her pistol toward Dan-Lee when he stopped suddenly and turned.

Dan-Lee smiled. "The ProConsul really hates both you."

Martin relaxed her body and lowered her pistol. "That's no big secret."

"Yes…but that's why when those rabid dogs she sent tried to kill the Council member I was guarding and I heard Scout Rangers were fighting with them, I figured I could use the Akota to get clear."

"Well…you got balls," replied Martin. "I'll give you that—wait…you were guarding a Council member?"

Dan-Lee smiled as he reached toward a panel on the bulkhead. He pulled the cover free, letting it fall onto the deck. Inside the small compartment was a man curled into the fetal position. His hands and feet bound and his mouth was gagged.

"Allow me to introduce Councilman Coppertree."

"No shit."

"Coppertree was one of the primary negotiators for the Council so he knows all sorts of things the Akota would be very interested in…deals the Association had with the Humani, deals with warlords and other leaders in the Dark Zone…and lots of other things."

Martin looked at the frightened man shoved into the little compartment. If half of what Dan-Lee said was true, this guy could help the Akota win the war. "Take him out."

"Hard to do like this," said Dan-Lee, holding his bound hands toward Martin.

"Fine." Martin holstered her sidearm and unlocked Dan-Lee's restraints. "Don't think I won't put a bullet in your brain if you try anything."

"Wouldn't expect anything less," replied Dan-Lee as he grabbed Coppertree by the collar and tossed him onto the deck.

Dan-Lee knelt down. "Knife?"

Martin let out a long sigh as she pulled a small, folding knife from her pocket and tossed it to Dan-Lee.

Dan-Lee opened the knife, no more than 5 centimeters long. "Really?"

"That will work," replied Martin. "You're fucking crazy if you think I'm giving you a real knife." She figured he had killed with far less anyway.

"Fine," grumbled Dan-Lee as he cut the restraints from Coppertree's ankles.

Coppertree tried to talk but all that escaped the gag was a series of grunts and groans.

"Shut up," ordered Dan-Lee as he bounced Coppertree's head off the deck.

"That's no way to treat your employer," said Martin with a smile.

"Trust me," said Dan-Lee as he looked up toward Martin. "He deserves far worse than he will get...than the rest of them got."

"We all deserve worse than we get," replied Martin.

Dan-Lee pulled Coppertree to his feet. "Maybe...but these Association assholes..." He shoved Coppertree in front of Martin. "Think of everything you have seen in the Dark Zone. The civil wars...the slave trade...the genocide...they profited from it all. Every family oppressed by a tyrant, every man forced to fight and die for another's gain..."

Dan-Lee gripped the back of Coppertree's neck.

Martin could see his hand tighten as Coppertree grunted against his grip.

"...and for every little girl ripped from her family and sold to satisfy old men's depravity," he continued. "...each time that happened, money went into this asshole's pocket."

Martin looked into Coppertree'e eyes. She looked beyond the terror to see the evil that lurked below. She wondered what someone who looked in her eyes would see.

"They're leeches that draw the lifeblood from the Dark Zone for their own enrichment. If I didn't need him, I'd kill him myself." He forced Coppertree to look into his eyes. "Slowly."

Martin took a deep breath. She knew Dan-Lee probably had ulterior motives and at some point may try to kill her or Stone. Everything about the situation told her to put a bullet in his brain. But something kept her from doing what she knew she should. "I know you have every right to want

190

vengeance on the First Families, and I honestly hope you get it. But I don't know what you expect from us."

"You can't trust me?" he laughed. "I bet you've been trying to decide whether or not to put a bullet in my brain the whole time."

"I...how can we trust you? Don't you remember our last meeting?"

"I do," he replied with a smile.

"Then what—how do you expect—"

"How many Akota have you killed?" he interrupted.

Martin remained silent.

"How many?"

Scenes from countless battles flashed before her. "I don't know."

"How many children have you left fatherless, Paladin Martin?"

Martin's stomach tightened; she didn't answer.

"How many children have you killed?"

"I don't know!" shouted Martin. "I don't know."

"But yet you work with the Akota?"

"They...they know who the true enemy is," snapped Martin.

"And how am I any different?"

"We didn't destroy their entire culture. I...uh..." Martin paused. She wished she hadn't said that.

"No, you didn't. But don't fool yourself; you would have if you had been able."

"Even then," replied Martin. "You know too much about what Stone and I have done…if I were you—"

"But I'm not you," interrupted Dan-Lee. "And don't underestimate yourselves. From listening to the Association talk about you, you two had already made a name for yourselves across the Dark Zone and with the Akota before this war started in proper fashion."

"What are you talking about?"

Dan-Lee chuckled. "I would have thought one of your new Akota friends would have told you."

"What the hell are you talking about?"

"Don't you know? To them you're the Humani angel of death."

"I know the Scout Ranger's knew of me. It makes—"

"Not the Rangers, all the Akota know about you."

"What?"

"Some Akota tell their children of the red-haired dragon that steals their fathers on the battlefield."

Martin stared at him blankly.

"What? You didn't know?"

An involuntary tear rolled down Martin's cheek but her expression remained unchanged. "I was doing my duty. I didn't know the Xen—"

"And now you know the truth," said Dan-Lee. "So if you trust a people that literally tell their children that you are a monster that destroys families, why can't you trust me?"

Martin remained silent, trying in vain to wash the girl's face from her mind.

"Just take him to Marshal Stone and he can decide what to do with him…and you."

Martin followed Dan-Lee as he walked Coppertree out of the transport. This time, however, she wasn't watching for any sudden movements. All she could think of was an Akota mother telling her child that she would never see their father again. She told herself everything she'd done was with her people in mind. Even though she was the arm of the evil intentions of the Xen and the First Families, her motivations had been noble. And she knew it.

But that Phelian girl haunted her. Despite how hard she tried—and how much she told herself it had to be done—she couldn't free herself from that day.

Then her thoughts flashed to what she had done to Maxa's wounded officers that dark, rainy night.

Before she realize it, they were standing in the hangar bay.

"Who is this?" asked Stone.

"This is the last surviving member of the Council," answered Martin.

Stone's eyes widened. "Are you sure?"

Martin glanced toward Dan-Lee. "Yes."

"Very well, then," said Stone, turning toward the lieutenant behind him. "Get this man to a security holding cell; a lot of people will want to talk to him."

"Yes, sir," replied the lieutenant, taking Coppertree from Dan-Lee. "And what about this one?"

Stone looked toward Dan-Lee then Martin. "What do we do with him?"

"Just an unmarked ship and my guns and knives," replied Dan-Lee, "and I'll be on my way."

Stone turned back to Dan-Lee. "If this guy pans out, you'll get your ship."

Chapter 11

Mori let out a grunt as she pushed her body to sprint through the last quarter of a kilometer. Each step sent pain coursing through her body and her knee felt like it would explode but she didn't stop...she couldn't. She focused on the distance reading and let out another loud grunt as she reached her mark.

Mori slowed the pace on the exercise platform that had been placed in her quarters for her rehabilitation.

She looked down at the display.

Ten kilometers in 35 standard minutes.

"Damn it," she cursed.

"That's still better than 85% of standard infantrymen," said the tech.

Mori slowed her pace further, placing her hands on her head to take in more air. "That," she huffed, "would be fine, corporal...if I were only an infantryman." She slowed her pace to a walk and tried to push the throbbing pain in her leg from her mind. "But I am Ki'etsenko."

"I understand, Ki'etsenko Ino'ka," said the tech. "And you'll be back to full speed soon. You're already so far ahead of schedule."

"It's not fast enough," grumbled Mori. Every minute she wasn't in the field was another minute Emily Martin was driving a wedge between her and Stone. "We'll go again tomorrow."

"You should wait at least two days for recovery," warned the tech. "Otherwise you could risk injury."

"Tomorrow." She gave the tech a stern look. "There's a lot more at stake than an injury." She hopped down from the platform onto the floor and let out a deep breath. "See, corporal, no problem."

"Yes, Ki'etsenko Ino'ka," replied the tech, clearly doubting her.

"That will be good for today," said Mori, letting the tech know it was time for him to leave.

"I'll see you tomorrow, Ki'etsenko Ino'ka," said the tech as he turned and left the room.

As the door slid shut, Mori let out a groan and collapsed into the chair behind her. "Damn it." She tried to rise again but fell back into the chair with a gasp as pain shot from her knee like a lightning bolt. Breathing heavily, she opened a small drawer in a table next to her chair.

Mori pulled a neuro-injector from the drawer, staring at it. "You're not going to get him," said Mori as she jabbed the injector into her thigh. She looked up toward the ceiling as she felt the pain begin to subside. After two heavy breaths she pushed herself off the chair.

196

The pain was still there, but manageable. She took a light step and quickly shifted her weight as the pain in her knee intensified.

"Shit."

Mori pulled another injector from the drawer and drove it into her thigh. She stood motionless for a moment, then took another step. "Better," she said aloud. Before the injury, two neuro-med injections would have clouded her mind and made it difficult to walk, but now...

She walked over to a cabinet next to her bed and pressed her hand against the security pad.

The cabinet opened, exposing several pistols, a tactical vest, a rifle, and her sword. She looked to the left, where Stone had kept his gear.

It was empty. He was...with her.

Mori pulled her shirt over her shoulders and grabbed a new one from the cabinet to the left of her weapons cache. She shoved her arms through the sleeves and pulled the shirt down over her torso. Next, she took a tunic from her cabinet, put it on, and began to button it. She looked back at the empty half of the gun cabinet. "Bitch," she said aloud before grabbing her sword and latching the belt around her waist. She then pulled a sidearm from the cabinet and slid it into place on her belt.

Maybe she couldn't run much more today but her trigger finger was just fine.

Mori took the rifle and slung it over her shoulder. "Range time," she said aloud. When her leg was finally healed, her other skills needed to be ready.

***

Stone sat at his desk in his stateroom onboard *Stormfall*, his body leaned backward and his head tilted toward the ceiling.

The mission had been a success; at least the Shirt-Wearers would see it that way. The Association was destroyed and, thanks to the Phelian Dan-Lee, they even had a captive with an incredible amount of intel on Humani interests, Dark Zone politics, and possibly even the Xen.

But three of his team had died and Katalya was devastated by the loss of Magnus. And there was the fact that Port Royal would fall to the Dorans, if it hadn't already.

He closed his eyes, trying to remember a time without death.

He couldn't.

Letting out a laugh of concession, he sat up straight in his chair.

A buzz on the panel on his desk let him know someone was outside.

He opened the door and Martin stepped through the door.

"Sir, I've come to give you a sitrep."

"Go ahead, Emily."

"Yes, sir. The Council member is locked up nice and cozy in security area 3. Orion and the engineer are checking over the ship for damage and rearming."

"And the rest of the team?"

"Shara is with Thay. The docs are still working on him; Shara will contact me if there is any news."

"And Katalya?"

"In her stateroom…she's not good."

"I wouldn't expect so. From what I know and what Mori has told me, this might be too much for her."

"She's strong," replied Martin. "She'll be okay."

"I hope so." He leaned back again, closing his eyes. Frustration washed over him and leaned forward, slamming his fist against the desk. "Three fucking dead."

"That's better than the thousands that would be dying on that moon right now, especially with the Dorans showing up." Martin placed her hands on Stone's desk and leaned in toward him. "You saved lives today, sir."

Stone sighed, his face still looking toward the desk. "Wouldn't it be great if just for once we had an outcome where no one dies?" He felt his teeth grinding. "Aren't you tired of trying to find the good in death?"

Martin pushed her body erect. "If you don't try…then what does that make us?"

"I guess you're right," replied Stone. "We're better—"

"Really, sir? What does that make us?"

He could see the frustration and anxiety on her face. "Emily?"

"Do you know the Akota tell stories about me to their children to scare them? They tell them I'm some kind of monster that takes their fathers from them."

"Sit," said Stone. He waited for Martin to lower herself into the chair on the other side of his desk. "Are you okay?"

"I…I'm fine, sir." she replied as she began to rise. "I shouldn't have—"

"Sit," ordered Stone.

"Really, sir. I'm—"

"Sit. Down." He waited for her to settle back into the chair. "How else would they look at us? We were their enemies." He leaned forward. "We thought no different of the Scout Rangers, especially the painted faces."

"Sir, I really don't want—"

"It's okay to feel, Emily," said Stone. "You can't always leave everything locked up inside. It's not a sign of weakness."

"That's very Akota of you," said Martin with a weak laugh, turning her head away from him. When she turned back, her face was flush. "When I killed, I did it because I believed I was fighting for my people. At least I used to…"

"But your reputation as a warrior never bothered you before?"

"And it still doesn't," snapped Martin. "But I'm a professional, not some fucking merc…or a monster."

"A professional soldier is still a monster to their enemy, Emily. We just don't usually end up living with our former enemies."

"You're right, sir," she replied. "Thank you for—"

"But the story-telling isn't what's bothering you, is it?"

"Sir?"

"Do you remember the first time you took a life?"

"Sir?"

"Do you?"

Martin sighed. "Yes."

"What do you remember about it?"

"I don't know what that has to do with anything?"

He had to get to her.

"What do you remember?"

"Fine," huffed Martin. "It was a Scout Ranger on Sierra 7."

"How?"

Martin twisted her body as she sat in the chair. "I killed him at 50 meters with my rifle."

"What else do you remember?"

"Nothing."

Stone stood and walked to the front of his desk and sat on the edge next to Martin. He knew where the source of her pain was, he just didn't know the details. "What about Golf 2?"

Martin's head shot up toward him. "What?"

"Tell me what happened."

He saw Martin tighten her body and turn away.

"It's okay. Tell me."

She turned back, tears rolling down her cheeks. "I can't."

He placed his hand on her shoulder. "You can...you need to."

Martin looked into his eyes but he could tell they were looking past him, as if she was watching something play out on a screen. "I was trying to find meds for...for Hugh," she said softly. "I found the old Terillian base but they'd taken it over."

"The Phel?"

"Yes. And I had to..." She paused, taking in a deep breath. "A lot of them were young."

"Tell me about the one you remember."

"I remember them all," she snapped.

"There's always one you remember," he confessed, with a slight crack in his voice.

"I…"

He knelt next to her. "Tell me."

"She was just a kid," mumbled Martin. "I didn't want to do it…I didn't even…" She wiped her cheeks. "I could see she hated me so much, just because I was Humani…but I didn't want to…" Unable to hold back, she began to sob.

Stone felt her lean toward him and took her in his arms. He ran his hand over her hair and turned her head so that he could look into her tear-soaked eyes. "And because you won't forget…that's why you're no monster."

She returned his gaze. "But I've done other things…I can feel the monster inside me, pushing against my soul. Sometimes it's all I can do to—"

Stone's stomach tightened as his mind drifted. "I was just a lieutenant and we were sent to the Foxtrot system to deal with a warlord that had been working with the Terillians. It took us about a week of working through small villages before we found out where he was hiding. The raid was quick and then we started a sweep for intel…"

"Sir?"

He didn't reply. His thoughts were on a faraway planet and years ago.

"Tyler?" Martin was almost whispering.

"We found a room…" He took a deep breath. "It was where the warlord kept his toys."

"Toys?"

"The dissenters he tortured…and…" He paused again. "There were close to a dozen young girls chained to beds in the room."

"Oh," replied Martin. "But that wasn't your—"

"There was this one girl…probably thirteen standard years…maybe," continued Stone. "She had these soft blue eyes and almost golden hair."

"But that's—"

"I remembered those eyes from a few days earlier when we passed through one of the villages under the warlord's control. I remembered because her father begged us to take the girl with us before the warlord's people took her." A weak laugh escaped him. "Of course I ignored him, just like every other time someone asked for something that the mission wouldn't support…besides, what the hell would we do with a little girl? She would have slowed us down and there wasn't anywhere for her to go…and she was just one of hundreds."

"But you saved her," said Martin. "He may have already…" She paused, "…but you saved her."

"No," replied Stone, swallowing hard. "I didn't. When the warlord…hell, I don't even remember his name…when he found out we were coming he…"

"He killed them." Martin was no stranger to what happened in the Dark Zone.

"Yes. He ordered all of them killed."

"What happened to him?"

"I pressed my pistol against his forehead and blew the back of his head off," said Stone. "But it didn't bring her back."

"You didn't have—"

"Amelia. That was her name," said Stone. "I have no idea why I remember it; like I said, she was one of hundreds. And I have seen far worse things in my years." It was now Stone who felt a tear rolling down his face. "But we don't pick the ones that will haunt us."

"Then what do we do about it?" asked Martin.

"We live...and we fight," replied Stone. "And we carry the pain—their pain—because we owe it to them and all of the other ones that don't stay with you."

He rose, pulling Martin with him. As they stood, Martin stepped back from their embrace.

"Thank you," said Martin as she looked up toward him, drying her eyes.

"Sooner or later we all need to talk about our *one*," said Stone. "For me, it took Sergeant Yates and a bottle of whiskey to get it out of me."

"Sergeant Yates?" Martin's thoughts drifted back to those dark days on Golf 2 and how much she had learned from Yates.

"Now there's a great soldier," said Stone as a small smile faded. "I wonder if I'll meet him in battle someday."

"You won't," replied Martin flatly.

"Why's that?"

"He's dead."

"Dead? What battle? When?"

"Just a few months after...after you left," said Martin. "He was killed in a training accident."

"A training accident?" Yates deserved a better death than that.

"He was transferred to train new infantry recruits and one of them inadvertently discharged his rifle and killed him."

"Son of a bitch," said Stone. "Killed by a recruit."

"Crazy times," replied Martin.

"Crazy times," repeated Stone.

After a long pause, Martin stood. "Thank you."

"For what?" asked Stone.

"Just for talking about...for listening."

Stone stood and walked over to Martin. "We all need someone to talk to sometimes...even the great Major Emily Martin."

"Yes, sir," replied Martin with a smile.

Stone looked into her eyes and returned the smile.

He realized his gaze was still locked onto hers but he couldn't turn away. He hadn't told the story about the girl to anyone since Yates so many years ago...but it felt right telling her. She, better than anyone, could understand.

Her eyes told him she felt the same way.

He raised her hand to Martin's face. "We're gonna be okay."

Martin closed her eyes as his hand pressed against her cheek. The softness of her skin sent a tingle down his spine.

Martin opened her eyes.

This time when their eyes met, she stepped away. "Sir, I..."

Stone dropped his hand and stepped back. The break of their contact brought him back to his senses. "Uh, yes..." he stammered. "I think we should call it a night."

"Yes, sir," she replied with an awkward smile. "I'll stop by Katalya and check on her."

"Thank you," replied Stone.

With a nod, Martin turned and almost sprinted out of his stateroom.

"Damn it," cursed Stone as the door closed. He had no idea what had caused him to put his hand to her cheek...and no idea why it felt the way it did.

***

Martin stood outside Katalya's stateroom, her hand centimeters from the announcing panel. Her mind raced and her stomach was tight as she thought back to her meeting with Stone. Normally, any feelings like that would have caused her to hit the gym, the range, or the bar…but she had told Stone she would talk to Katalya. It was the first thing she could think of to get out of his stateroom and the awkward moment they had shared.

She took a deep breath and pressed the panel.

The door slid open.

"Katalya?" asked Martin as she looked inside the room.

There was no reply.

"Katalya?"

Martin stepped into the room. "Marshal Stone wanted me to—" She paused when she saw Katalya setting on the edge of her bed, her head in her hands. "Can I get you anything?"

Katalya slowly raised her head to show a tear-soaked face. "Yes…I would like Magnus back…or my children," she snapped. "Can you get that for me?"

Martin exhaled, closing her eyes briefly. She may not have experienced everything Katalya had, but she knew what it meant to lose someone you loved. "No, I can't." She walked over to Katalya and knelt in front of her. "We can't bring back the ones we've lost."

"I have nothing left."

"That's not true," replied Martin. "You have your sister...and..."

"Why are you trying to...why are *you* here?" said Katalya.

"I told Marshal Stone I would check on you," asked Martin. "To see if you were okay..."

'Of course she's not okay,' thought Martin as soon as she said the words.

Katalya guffawed. "What do you think?"

"I...I just..."

"You suck at this," said Katalya.

Of course Katalya was right, but Stone had gotten her off her game and now she was stuck talking feelings with Katalya. "We both know this isn't my thing but I'm here..." She paused. "Look, I won't claim to know what's going through your mind right now but I know what it's like to hurt so much that it feels like your stomach is on fire and you can't breathe because every breath reminds you that you're alive and someone you love isn't."

"When I met Magnus, I was ready to die," said Katalya. "I'd fought so hard as a slave in the Dark Zone just to stay alive and for a moment..." Tears began to flow again. "...for a moment, I had everything I wanted but slavers ripped that from me..."

Katalya stopped and lowered her head, unable to speak.

Martin placed her hand on Katalya's knee. "I'm not gonna try to say some bullshit that will make you feel better…" Martin's thoughts went to the sight of her father as he died. "…but I will gladly help you take your revenge on the ones that have done this."

Katalya looked up toward Martin. "That…and pain are all I have left."

"Let that pain turn to hate," said Martin. "It works for me."

***

"Is he ready?" asked Stone.

"Yes, Marshal Stone," replied the security officer.

"And the man that brought him?"

"Intel verified the guy in there is a Council member and per your orders, we returned the other man's weapons and he left on an old transport we had confiscated in a previous raid."

"Very well," said Stone, "let's see what the Councilman has to say."

Stone nodded and a guard opened the door to Councilman Coppertree's holding cell.

Stone walked into the room and sat across from Coppertree. He took a moment to look over the man. Coppertree's attire or physical features were unimportant; his physique was soft and he was dressed in the leather and brass-accessorized outfits common to all Association members, but what mattered were his eyes.

Fear.

He wouldn't need much convincing.

"Do you know what has happened to the Association...to the council members?"

"I don't have to answer any of your questions," replied Coppertree, his voice cracking. "Both the Akota and the Humani have violated the terms of—"

"You do understand your diplomatic duplicity won't work," interrupted Stone. "The days of the Association playing both sides of the fence are over...because there is no more Association."

"I don't believe you."

"You know who attacked you...what they were. And you know who we are." He leaned forward. Again Coppertree's eyes betrayed him. "Alright. Now that that is settled, we can have a conversation."

"I'll want some assurances," replied Coppertree. "And it won't be cheap."

"I don't think you understand your situation, Councilman."

"I think I do," replied Coppertree as Stone noticed a small, unsure smile start to form. "If the Humani had taken me, they would torture me…but you are Akota now and the Akota—"

Coppertree paused and his eyes widened as the door behind Stone opened.

Stone turned to see Martin step into the room and lean against the wall.

He turned back toward Coppertree; the flash of confidence had faded from his face.

"So you were saying something about not being tortured," said Martin with a glance toward Stone. "Last time I checked, I'm not Akota."

"I take it you know who my friend here is?" asked Stone.

Coppertree locked his gaze on Stone, purposely avoiding Martin's stare. "I do."

"Good," said Martin. "Then I'll make a deal with you." She pressed her back off from against the wall. "Either you answer Marshal Stone's questions…or we'll have to chat," she added as she played with a knife drawn from her vest.

"So who do you want to talk to, Councilman…me or Major Martin?"

"What do you want to know?" asked Coppertree.

"Good choice," said Martin as she pressed her hands against the desk, leaning forward toward Coppertree. "If you don't answer every single question, I'm coming back. Do you understand?"

Coppertree averted his gaze from Martin and nodded.

"Look at me!" shouted Martin, causing Coppertree to almost jump out of his chair. "Do you understand?"

"Yes," mumbled Coppertree.

"Good," said Martin as she stood. "Easy peasy," she added with a smile.

As she turned to exit the room, Stone saw her smile fade. Her reputation might be useful, but Stone wondered how it now weighed on her after their conversation.

The door closed behind Martin and Stone returned his focus to Coppertree.

"What do you know about Dolus?"

"Everything," replied Coppertree.

"How severely was the station damaged in the attack?"

"It took significant damage but Astra Varus has doubled her efforts after placing Alpha Humana under martial law. With complete control of the Humani government and the Dorans more involved in the Dark Zone, the Dolus project is almost back on track to have the fleet and army ready when virus takes effect."

"How far along has the development of the virus come?"

"You don't know?"

"You don't get to ask the questions," replied Stone, his concern growing.

"It is fully developed and the first shipment of slaves with the genetic coding have already been shipped to Xen worlds."

Stone leaned forward. "It's started?"

Coppertree laughed. "Yes, but ProConsul Varus is smart…and patient when it comes to her plans for conquest."

"What do you mean?"

"The virus won't begin to spread for a decade at the earliest. That is the beauty of the plan; when the children of those infected reach puberty, it will wash over the Xen planets like a tsunami."

Stone sat back in his chair. He wasn't sure which would be worse, a galaxy under control of the Xen or Astra. "And the Dark Zone?"

"Not yet," said Coppertree. "If she were to use the virus in the Dark Zone first, she would run the risk of alerting her allies of its existence."

Stone knew Astra wouldn't wait too long. She would want the Akota and any Dark Zone resistance weakened soon after the Xen were weakened in order to allow her to focus on her former masters without fear of losing ground against the Akota. "How long until it is released in the Dark Zone?"

"I don't know."

Stone slammed his fist against the table and grabbed Coppertree's shirt, pulling him out of the chair onto the table. "Don't lie to me!"

"I don't know!" pleaded Coppertree. "I don't know."

Stone released Coppertree and let him fall back into his chair.

"Astra Varus only told us what we needed to know to carry out her plans."

"Has it started?"

"I don't think so," replied Coppertree. "I would guess you have nine standard months...maybe a year."

"I am assuming she has an antivirus?"

"She does."

"Where is it?"

"Dolus."

Stone's jaw tightened. "Who else has it?"

"I don't know but she will no doubt be in the process of inoculating her troops."

"What about the formula? Who knows how to make it?"

"Our scientists developed the virus and antivirus."

Stone let out a heavy sigh. "Which is now under control of the Dorans." He noticed a curl in Coppertree's mouth. "Or is it?" Stone leaned closer. "Where are your scientists?"

"We have a station in the nebula beyond the Juliet system."

"There's nothing out there...no stars...nothing."

"That's why it was chosen."

"What kind of security does it have?"

"Association forces…maybe 250 security forces with a small contingent of fighters."

"Does Astra know its location?"

"I don't think so. If she does…"

"It's already destroyed," said Stone. If it wasn't, the station could hold the key to saving billions and stopping Astra Varus from galactic domination.

Stone rose from his chair and turned toward the door.

"Don't you want to know more…our accounts, trade contacts, the—"

"I'll leave that to the Akota," interrupted Stone. He had to get to that station…and he had to do it soon.

As the door opened, Stone saw Martin standing in the passageway. Her face was tight and her mouth thin with frustration.

"What is it?"

"Thay's dead."

***

Stone stared at the group in front of him. The deaths of the Akota Ki'etsenkos, Magnus, and now Thay weighed heavy on his heart and as he looked at Martin, Shara, and Katalya. The three sat around the small table in his stateroom; all of them were emotionally exhausted.

He noticed the light on his panel and opened the door.

Orion walked into the room, followed by Rickover. As they took their seats, he could see they felt it too.

"So what's the next plan?" asked Orion.

"Find that fucking bitch and kill her," replied Katalya.

"Katalya's right," added Martin.

"We have another mission first," replied Stone.

Katalya rose from the table. "We're not going after them?"

He could see the group react in unison, their bodies shifting in surprise.

"Sir?" asked Martin. "Thay..." She glanced toward Katalya. "Magnus...she killed them. We need—"

Stone raised his hand to silence Martin. "I understand. And her day will come but we have to look toward the greater good."

"What's more important than making that bitch bleed?" snapped Katalya.

"Saving millions, maybe billions from death and enslavement by Astra Varus," replied Stone. "She's already released the virus on the Xen and will probably release it into the Dark Zone and against the Akota within the year."

"It's started?" asked Orion, sitting upright in her chair.

"It's designed to take a long time to activate...to allow Astra's army and fleet on Dolus to be completed. We probably have a standard decade."

"Ten years?" asked Shara.

"It's embedded in the slaves being sent to the Xen but their offspring will actually release the virus."

"Brilliant," mouthed Rickover. "So slow as to not be noticed initially, even if a few cases occur early, but once it gains momentum...it will cripple the Xen."

"Astra Varus is no fool when it comes to conquest," said Martin.

"How can it be stopped?" asked Shara.

"The Association has a science station beyond the Juliet system where the virus was developed. They have the antivirus."

"And that's where we're going?" asked Orion.

"Yes," said Stone. "If Astra hasn't found out about it and destroyed the station already."

"And if she has?" asked Martin.

"Then she might just win," answered Stone flatly.

"When are we leaving?"

"I've sent an electron spin message to the Shirt-Wearers. We'll transfer to the heavy cruiser *Yellow Star* and transit to the edge of the Juliet system. Two platoons of Scout Rangers will rendezvous with us. The cruiser will have enough firepower and fighter support to deal with their defenses while we board them."

Chapter 12

"It's good to see you again, Uncles," said Mori as she stood before the Shirt-Wearers.

Her leg still ached but it wasn't going to stop her from getting back to full duty.

"We are glad to see you, Ino'ka," said Shirt-Wearer River.

"We have followed your recovery and have been impressed with your effort," added Shirt-Wearer Wolf.

"I can't sit by while the fate of my people is at stake," replied Mori.

"And how can you best serve your people, Ino'ka?" asked River.

"Uncle?"

"What is your path?" added Wolf.

"My path is whatever my people need it to be." She meant it, but a knot formed in her stomach.

"We have discussed your destiny amongst ourselves and with the wichasa wakhan," said River.

The knot tightened. "And what is it the nation needs me to do?"

"Sit, Ino'ka," said Wolf as he motioned toward a wooden chair with fur backing.

"At the table, Uncle?"

"Yes...sit," repeated Wolf.

It was an honor to sit with the Shirt-Wearers…an honor well below her rank and status. Taking a deep breath, Mori lowered herself into the chair. The creak of the chair broke the silence like a gunshot.

She took another breath.

"We and the wichasa wakhan believe you will someday sit at this table permanently," said Shirt-Wearer Shadow. "Is that what you want?"

"If it is for the good of our people," she replied. She felt it was her destiny but showing too much ambition for such a position was a sure way to never achieve it. But they did ask her. "I have sensed it may be my destiny…but that is not for me to decide. I can only serve my people and let my fate be determined by my service."

"Well said, Ino'ka," said River. "That is why we have asked you here…to see if you are ready to serve your people instead of your ambitions."

"I am, Uncle."

"What do all of the current and previous Shirt-Wearers have in common?" asked Wolf.

"They were men," she said instinctively. But that wasn't what they were asking and she knew it.

"What else?" asked Falling-rock, repositioning himself in his chair.

"They were generals, admirals, or spiritual leaders."

"Yes," said River. "And you are neither."

"I…"

"It's okay," interrupted River, raising his hand. "We understand you are still young…as were we at one point."

"Yes, Uncle?"

"So you must reach flag rank or be initiated into the wichasa wakhan," answered Wolf.

Mori tilted her head. She would never be balanced enough to be a spiritual leader.

"So flag rank it is," added Wolf.

"But the Rangers—"

"That is why you will be reassigned to the regular Akota army and given the rank of Ate second grade in the Akota records and Colonel in the unified Terillian structure," said River.

Mori's mind raced. It was clearly what they thought she needed to become a Shirt-Wearer, but she had always been a Ranger. "Thank you, Uncles," she replied. "Can I ask—"

"You will still retain the rank of Ki'etsenko, but the people must come to know you as a leader instead of a fighter."

"Yes, Uncle." Mori's anxiousness faded as she began to see the path to her destiny grow clearer.

"But you will have one more mission with the Rangers," said River.

"I am ready," replied Mori.

"Pick two platoons from 2nd Regiment. You will rendezvous with Marshal Stone and his team to attack an Association science station that may hold the antivirus formula."

Mori's excitement faded as she realized she would need to have yet another painful discussion with Stone.

"Is everything okay, Ino'ka?" asked Wolf.

"Uh...yes, Uncle."

"Magakisca frustrates the clarity of your vision?" asked River.

"He does," confessed Mori. "I have spoken with the wichasa wakhan on many occasions but it is all clouded. I feel like he is part of my destiny but it...it is very hard." She exhaled heavily. "Sometimes I—"

"What will happen will happen," interrupted River. "The relationship between Magakisca and you will be an important one for our people; that is clear to the wichasa wakhan. What is not clear is what that relationship will be."

"But what must be certain is where your loyalty lies, Ino'ka," said Wolf. "If you must choose, do you chose a seat on this council...or Magakisca?"

Mori froze. It was the question she'd fooled herself into thinking she wouldn't have to answer.

"Ino'ka?" repeated Wolf.

"The council," she exhaled, forcing the truth from her mouth.

"Good," said Falling-rock. "Then we have specific orders for you when the station is taken."

"What is it?"

"The antivirus may be on the station, or at least the formula," said River. "If it is there, you need to secure it and return it here to us."

"Of course, Uncle...but wouldn't Maga—"

"Magakisca is a great war leader," said River, "and his heart drives him to do what is right, but..."

"He may have Akota blood and may still become a full member of our nation but his sympathies are easily swayed toward the Hanmani or the Dark Zone populations," said Wolf. "And we need to make sure we have control of the antivirus so our scientists can replicate and produce the antivirus...with our military being the first to be vaccinated."

"Of course," replied Mori.

"You must understand, Ino'ka," said River, leaning toward Mori, "that is why you are being sent on this mission...Magakisca cannot distribute the vaccine to the Dark Zone before our troops are inoculated. It is both a matter of preparedness and strategy."

"Strategy."

"If disease spreads to the Dark Zone, the Humani will assume it has spread to us as well and will commit armies against a force they believe to be weakened, if not decimated," said River.

"It will be a huge advantage for us," added Falling-rock.

"And those in the Dark Zone?"

"Many may still survive," said River. "It is unfortunate as they are Akota by blood...but we must ensure we survive in order to help them in the end."

Mori closed her eyes. Her people had to come first, despite the cost. She opened her eyes and exhaled again...there was no way Stone would accept it.

"Do you understand your orders, Ino'ka?" asked Wolf.

"I do."

"Will you carry them out...for the Akota people?" asked River.

"I will."

***

Sierra grunted as she walked down the passageway of the Doran cruiser toward the captain's stateroom. It had only been a week since she was wounded in the fight at Port Royal but her healing had progressed quickly. She wouldn't be fully recovered for weeks but she could walk...as long as she could take the pain.

"Halt!" ordered a Doran guard standing outside the captain's stateroom.

"Commander Skye, representing the ProConsul Astra Varus of Alpha Humana to see Captain Veri."

The guard stepped to the side as the door opened.

Sierra stopped as she reached the door, turning toward the guard. "What is your rank?"

"I am a 3rd line shield warrior."

"So you are not an officer?"

"I am not."

"I am an officer and as an ally in the Xen Empire, you will afford me the same respect as one of your officers," she said, stepping in close to the guard.

The tall guard turned his head downward toward her, his eyes covered by the bluish hue of his helmet visor.

Sierra stared into the blue glow, unwilling to yield.

After a long pause, the guard stepped back and brought his right hand to his chest.

"That's better," said Sierra as she turned and stepped into the stateroom.

"Commander Skye," said Captain Veri from behind his desk.

"Captain," replied Skye, rendering a Doran salute. "Request to enter."

Captain Veri motioned for her to enter.

Sierra dropped her salute and stepped to the edge of the large metallic desk with purple cloth draped over the sides. "You wanted to speak to me?"

"Yes, Commander," replied Veri. "As you can guess, our intelligence teams are going through the Association files."

"Yes, sir," replied Sierra. "What does that mean to me?"

"Prince Vali has directed that you be informed of any information related to scientific research...your ProConsul is concerned the Association was selling Humani technology to the Akota."

Sierra knew that was not true; Astra Varus would have had the Council destroyed earlier if she felt they were betraying any real secrets. Why would Astra Varus ask the Dorans to share this information? "What is the intel, sir?"

"We found information about an Association research station in the nebula beyond the Juliet system."

"Do you have any other information?"

"Just that it exists and the vector coordinates. There are also communications between the Council and the station but they have not been decrypted yet."

"So there is a science station beyond the Juliet system...and that is all you have?"

"Yes...it was your ProConsul that requested the information, Commander."

"I understand, captain," replied Sierra. "Is there anything else?"

"That will be all, Commander Skye."

"Aye, sir," replied Sierra with another Doran salute. She turned to exit.

"Commander," said Veri.

"Sir?" asked Sierra, turned back toward the captain.

"How long will you and your men remain here?"

"Until we are directed by the ProConsul to leave," replied Sierra. "Which I'm guessing will be soon after I relay this message to her."

***

Sierra activated the electron spin signal and anxiously awaited the response. She had prostrated herself, at least through message traffic, to the ProConsul in every communication she'd sent since Port Royal fell, but no angry backlash had come. Maybe this would be the time.

The light above the screen marked 'incoming message' flashed green.

Sierra took a deep breath and hit 'receive'. She read the message.

Proceed to Association science station with your team. Take the station and destroy any material associated with the 'Project Dominotra'. Do not forget your primary objective is to capture either of the Traitors, alive if possible, if they are present.

"At least I can kill one of them," said Sierra to herself.

"Why does she want them alive?" asked Lieutenant Kawal.

"The only thing more important to the ProConsul than ensuring the Traitors are brought to justice is getting her son back."

"Even if she finds out where he is, he will be most likely be deep in enemy territory."

"I don't think she will care, Lieutenant," replied Sierra. "She'll do whatever it takes to get him back." She stood and turned toward Kawal. "And you shouldn't get in the habit of questioning the ProConsul's orders, Lieutenant."

"I wasn't...of course, Commander."

"What is our current strength?"

"We have thirty ready for duty."

"Then get them ready," ordered Sierra as she turned away from Kawal. "We'll sacrifice everything to capture one of them."

***

The tunic of Stone's dress uniform pressed against his neck as he awaited the Iroqua party. With Thay's death, word had been sent to the clan matrons and they had sent a party to retrieve his body so that their customs may be carried out. The request by the clan matrons had delayed their jump to the rendezvous point to pick up the Scout Rangers that would join them on the attack on the science station, but no one would challenge a request by the matrons, given their political influence in the Terillian Confederation.

Stone and his team stood in the ceremonial reception room onboard *Yellow Star*. He turned back toward Martin and Shara, standing in formation behind him. Like him, they wore their full dress Humani uniforms modified with a red rope braid over the left shoulder to signify their rebellion against the First Families and the ProConsul.

Behind Martin and Shara stood Orion and Katalya.

Orion wore her ceremonial uniform, consisting of red breechcloth worn over her dress trousers and tucked under her ceremonial belt which held her sidearm and an ornate knife. Her hair was still curled but an eagle feather was affixed to her hair and fell against her cheeks.

Katalya wore a plain tactical uniform but her hair was tied into two braided tails that extended forward over her shoulders to her waist. Stone couldn't help but notice the pain still painted on her face.

Next to Stone stood Commander Eagleheart, *Yellow Star's* commanding officer.

"As senior officer, you will need to greet them first, Marshal," whispered Eagleheart. "There is no special greeting...just introduce yourself and state that you were his war leader."

Stone nodded in acknowledgment just before his attention was drawn to the opposite side of the room as the large double-doors slid open.

As the doors opened, four large warriors stepped into the room, each wore buckskin leggings and black breechcloths over their trousers. They were shirtless, displaying well-muscled but lean torsos. The warriors' upper torsos were painted black, with the paint extending upward to their jaws. The rest of their faces were painted dull red which also covering their bald heads. Each ear had a bone earring and a single feather was attached to the lone tuft of hair positioned just a little back from the top of their heads.

The four warriors stopped, two on each side and turned toward the center.

Behind them came an Iroqua dressed in black leggings with a long buckskin over-shirt that fell below his waist. In one hand was a turtle shell and another a dark brown hide of a small animal. The Iroqua's face was covered with a wooden mask painted red, black, and white with long lengths of weaved grass protruding from the back.

The masked man walked past the other warriors and then stopped and knelt.

The warriors lowered their heads as a small woman walked into the room.

She wore red cloth shoes with white trimming and brown trousers. A large blue blanket was draped over her torso and came down to her knees. Her face was devoid of any makeup or paint and her dark, black hair was tied into a single braid that fell down her back. Shifting back to her face, he could make out loose wrinkles around her eyes and on her brow. He also made out small traces of grey in her hair.

She had to be the senior member.

Stone stepped forward.

"I am Marshal Stone. I was Thayendanegea's leader."

The woman looked up toward Stone, her wrinkled face tense. "I am Onatah, of the Wolf Clan...and you are the Humani who defied your ProConsul?"

"I am," he replied.

"Thayendanegea's way, while always honoring his clan, was his own. Many doubted the prudence of fighting with the Akota but once he declared mourning war, no one would challenge him."

Stone was not sure if she was saying Thay shouldn't have fought with the Akota—and especially him—or if she was praising his drive.

"Thayendanegea was a brave warrior. His enemies never saw his back," said Martin, in Iroqua, as she stepped next to Stone. She gave Stone a glance before continuing. "I am Major Emily Martin—"

231

"Red Wolf," interrupted the woman.

The Iroqua warriors' heads snapped toward the direction of Martin, who held her gaze on the woman.

"Yes."

"Thayendanegea spoke of you…first of his desire to kill you…then of his respect for your loyalty and skill."

"A compliment from a warrior such as him is an honor," replied Martin.

The woman gave Martin a nod and turned toward Stone again.

"May I see him?" she asked.

"Of course," replied Stone and motioned for two guards to open the door behind Shara, Orion, and Katalya.

The doors opened and four Akota in full dress uniform slowly carried a wooden platform with Thay's body.

Stone could see Thay's arms folded over his body, with a tomahawk in each hand, as tradition dictated.

As the platform moved past Stone's team, he saw Katalya's face grow red as her breathing grew more labored. Suddenly, she turned and rushed from the room.

"She is in mourning," said Stone.

"Many mourn nowadays," said Onatah.

"Did you know Thayendanegea?" asked Stone.

Again the woman looked up, her eyes wet with tears. "He is my son."

Stone's knees almost gave out. "Your son?"

"Yes," she replied. "That is why I must speak with your Red Wolf."

Stone turned toward Martin. He could see the shock on her face.

"Come here," said Onatah, motioning for Martin.

Martin slowly walked up to the woman, who stood next to Thay's body as the Akota warriors lowered the platform to the deck.

"You do understand Thayendanegea came to fight in this war to avenge the life you took."

"I do," replied Martin.

"And now my family again faces death."

Martin stood silently.

"Do you understand what this means?"

Stone's body tensed as he began to contemplate just how bad this could be.

"I do. And I will tell you that your son stopped being an enemy of mine long ago. He is...was a brother in arms, fighting against the true evil in this galaxy."

Stone had never known Martin to be so conciliatory, but he was sure even she knew the power of the woman she was talking to...as well as the level of her pain.

Onotah knelt next to Thay and placed her hand on his forehead.

With a heavy exhale, she rose and turned toward Martin.

"Red Wolf, what do you feel about my son's death?"

"Anger...no rage," she replied. "I want to hold the heart of the one that did this in my hand."

Onatah nodded in acknowledgment. "Then please kneel."

Martin looked toward Stone.

He motioned for her to kneel and gave her a nod.

Martin knelt in front of the grieving Iroqua matron.

Onatah placed her hand on Martin's shoulder.

"It is the belief of our people that the spirit of a warrior, if they have a good death, will be passed into the body of another. My son spoke to me before he returned about you."

Stone jerked as the Onatah landed an open hand against Martin's cheek.

Martin looked up toward the woman, her eyes wide. But she did not react.

"Despite the pain you have caused this family, he told me that your heart was that of a warrior. Was he right?"

"Yes," replied Martin, her left cheek now bright red.

"Then rise, Awaheya, daughter of the wolf clan."

Martin looked toward Stone and then back toward Onatah.

"Rise," said the matron.

Martin rose to her feet. "I don't—"

"My son told me that if he were to die that you should be the one to exact vengeance for our family."

"That I will do, Onatah," replied Martin. "But I am Humani, not Iroqua."

"That does not matter, Awaheya." Onatah reached down and pulled one of the tomahawks from Thay's hand and extended it toward Martin. "You owe the Iroqua nothing but to be the warrior that you are…and make Thayendanegea's tomahawk wet with blood again."

Martin took the tomahawk from Onatah. "That I can promise you."

Onatah then turned toward Stone. "My son's mourning is over and his war will be continued by Awaheya." She stepped toward Stone. "But my heart is still heavy…so the Iroqua will go to war against the Humani."

"You are entering the war?"

"It is my right to ask this of the council…and they will not refuse."

"Thank you," replied Stone.

"Do not thank me, Humani," said Onatah. "My son was right to fight this evil and I have paid for my unwillingness to aid my Akota brothers with his death. I will withhold this aid no longer. The Shirt-Wearers and the Terillian Council Lodge have been informed of our entry in the war."

She turned back toward Martin.

"But your war is with the one that took my son…that is your oath to me."

"And one I will gladly take," replied Martin.

Onatah motioned for the four warriors and they moved toward her, each grabbing an edge of the platform and lifting Thay's body into the air. Another motion and the warriors began to exit with Thay's body, the medicine man walking slowly behind them, chanting in Iroqua.

"Thank you for allowing my son to die among such brave warriors," said Onatah. "Now I must return to my clan."

Onatah turned and began to walk away.

"Onatah," asked Martin.

"Yes?" she asked turning back toward Martin.

"The name you gave me, Awaheya…what does it mean?"

A tight smile came to Onatah's face. "Death."

Chapter 13

Sierra stood on the deck of the battle cruiser *Ragna* next to the ship's captain.

"We are prepared for our jump, Commander Skye," reported Captain Vaal.

"Excellent," replied Sierra. "Once we arrive, keep their defenses occupied. The company of Elite Guard and my men will board the station."

"Yes, commander," replied Vaal. "But wouldn't it be easier to just destroy the station with our guns?"

"If that was the ProConsul's wishes, Captain. But what she wishes is that we take the station and wait for the Akota to attack. I need the Traitors to enter the station so once you have destroyed their fighters you need to pull back out of range until I signal you. Once you receive the signal, jump back and engage whatever force they have sent."

"Yes, commander."

"And you, Major Richter," said Sierra, turning toward the Elite Guard major. "You're men will focus on their security forces and then take out any aircraft still in the hangars."

"We know our assignment, commander," grumbled Richter. "We are Guardsmen after all. I just want a shot at the Traitors."

Sierra moved close to Richter. "Do not forget, Major. One of them must be taken alive." She focused on the major's eyes. "And Martin is mine."

***

Stone stood like a statue as four long-range transports drifted toward the deck of *Yellow Star's* hangar bay. After the Iroqua funeral party had departed with Thay's body, *Yellow Star* had jumped to the designated rendezvous point with the Scout Rangers. As the transports locked into place, Stone exhaled heavily.

Mori was on one of those transports.

Stone's heart raced with an uncomfortable mixture of anticipation and anxiety as he watched the Rangers exit the transports.

Then he saw her.

Mori hopped from the troop compartment onto the deck, displaying a slight grimace before she moved to the front of her officers. Her braided hair swung behind her as she looked over her officers. Even though she hadn't looked toward Stone, he could see the brilliant flash of green in her eyes as she addressed her officers.

"Get your men settled and your gear stowed," she ordered. "I will brief you on the underway schedule at 1800 standard hours."

Unlike a Humani formation, there was no formal 'dismissed'; the officers simply began to scatter and attend to their men. As the group dispersed, Mori turned toward Stone.

Their eyes met and his stomach tightened. Mori's mouth curved into a smile. He moved toward her, picking up his pace as he grew closer. Just as he was about to reach her, he opened his arms to embrace her.

But he stopped in his tracks when Mori snapped to attention and rendered a Humani salute.

Stone returned the salute, but his stomach churned. "Major," he said, unsure of what to do next.

"Marshal Stone," replied Mori. "It's good to see you again." She moved in close to him. "I really missed you, Magakisca," she said softly.

Mori could see the confusion Stone was failing to hide.

"I thought you would prefer a salute in public," continued Mori. "I just—"

"I missed you, too," interrupted Stone as he took Mori in his arms. "And this feels much better than a salute."

The pressure of her body against his and feel of her hair against his cheek caused him to close his eyes as he tried to lock the moment into his memory. "I really did miss you."

"Me too," replied Mori, looking up toward him. "And its colonel," she added.

"Colonel?" Stone loosened his embrace to look into her eyes. "Did something happen to Colonel Rain or Blackriver?"

"No," chuckled Mori.

"Then how—"

"After this mission I will take command of the 5th Heavy Infantry Regiment."

"A line command?" Stone's memory flashed to his own promotion to colonel and the destruction of his regiment on Juliet 3.

"It's a stepping stone to—"

"Shirt-Wearer," said Stone.

"Is that a problem?" snapped Mori, stepping away from Stone's embrace.

"No." Stone backpedaled. "I'm happy for you."

"For us," replied Mori.

Stone wanted to be happy about Mori's promotion. But it only made him more anxious.

"That's great," said Stone, faking it. But Mori's gaze told him she didn't completely believe him.

"Are you okay?" she asked.

He wasn't. But he would tell her the part of the problem that didn't involve. He let out a sigh. "Port Royal was tough."

"How is Katalya?" Mori's jaw tightened as the concern for her sister overtook her thoughts.

"Not good," replied Stone. "We tried—"

"Where is she? I need to see her."

Stone could see the guilt painted on Mori's face for not going straight to her sister after landing.

"I can take you to her."

The short walk from the hangar to Katalya's stateroom was filled with silence as Stone tried to think of something to say. Mori remained silent as well, her focus set forward as she followed Stone through the ship. In a few awkward moments they reached a long row of doors at one of the sections of staterooms onboard *Yellow Star*. "Martin has been checking in—"

"Martin!" Mori's head swung toward Stone. "Why would you have that—" Mori paused. "Nevermind...which room is hers?"

Stone walked past three doors, stopping at the fourth on the right. "Here."

Mori pushed past Stone and knocked on the door.

The door slowly opened. Katalya's tired eyes opened wide when she saw her sister at the door.

"Kat?" said Mori softly.

Katalya's face slacked and tears began to fall down her cheeks. "He's gone," wailed Katalya as she collapsed into Mori's arms.

"I'm here for you, c'uwé," said Mori as she ran her hand over her sister's hair.

"I—"

"I'll meet with you after I talk with my sister, Marshal," said Mori, her eyes welling up from a combination of pain for her sister and anger. "Maybe you should go see your Chief of Staff...I'm sure she has nothing better to do than sit around waiting on you."

Stone's skin grew hot but knew it wasn't the right time to fight...for Katalya's sake. "I'll be waiting," he said flatly.

***

Stone sat alone in the silence of the briefing room, lost in thought. After Mori had returned from her time with Katalya, they did the only thing they seemed to be good at together. Afterwards, however, he spent a restless night as he wondered what would be the catalyst for their next argument.

Then the catalyst entered the room.

Emily Martin strode into the briefing room but paused when she saw Stone. "Sir?" Her mouth curled, puzzled at this presence. "The brief doesn't start for another ten min—"

"Don't let me bother you, Emily," replied Stone. He knew she would be the first in the room. "I just needed to get out of my office."

"Yes, sir," said Martin as she began to activate the holographic panels for the briefing to make sure they were correct. "Looks like Echo system is heating up again," she continued as she flipped through various displays.

"It looks like the Humani are trying to step up resistance, even if it means stirring up the Followers of the Word."

"Those fanatics are a problem for everyone." Martin paused in contemplation. "But Astra Varus would burn down the whole system if she thought she could gain from it."

Stone nodded in agreement. "I wouldn't be surprised if we end up back there again."

Martin looked up from her displays. "I already started developing op plans," she said with a smile.

Stone's attention was drawn toward Shara, Orion, and Rickover as they walked into the room. The absence of Magnus and Thay weighed heavy on him.

"Sir," said Shara as the group passed Stone toward their seats.

Stone replied with a nod.

Yellow Star's command officer, executive officer, and combat systems officer entered next. Behind them was the ship's senior flight officer.

"Good morning, Marshal Stone," said Commander Eagleheart.

"Captain," replied Stone, offering the title due to all commanding officers of vessels. As the fleet officers took their seats, Stone looked at his watch. It was time to—

Just as the meeting was scheduled to start, Mori entered the room with five of her officers. Next to Mori, as she stormed into the room, was Katalya.

"Ki'etsenko Skye, we are pleased to have you onboard," said Commander Eagleheart.

Stone figured he knew of Mori's promotion and her fast track toward becoming a Shirt-Wearer.

"Commander," replied Mori as she sat next to Stone. "Marshal," she said as she turned toward Stone. She cast a guilty smile toward him. "I hope you got enough sleep. I—"

"Now that everyone is here," interrupted Martin, her gaze locked on Mori, "Are you ready to begin, sir?"

"Let's begin," replied Stone.

"Yes, sir," replied Martin as she activated the first hologram. "Here's the section of the nebula where the Association station is expected to be. Based on intel received from the captured Council member, we believe the station has approximately 250 security forces and maybe ten older fighters."

"Our detachment of foxtrots should take care of the fighter," replied Orion.

"The station will have some close-defense systems," continued Martin, "but we should expect minimal resistance for our boarding ships. Once we board, the Rangers should secure the forward and aft approaches to the lab area and the primary assault team made up of Marshal Stone, First Sergeant Shara, Th—," Martin let out a heavy breath. "First Sergeant Shara, myself, and three Rangers picked by Major Sk—"

"Myself, Katalya, and Sergeant Meadow," interrupted Mori. "And it's colonel."

Martin positioned herself in front of Mori. Stone could see Martin's anger start to boil up from deep inside. He prepared himself so that he could respond to her reaction.

"Of course, colonel," replied Martin slowly.

Stone glanced toward Mori, her eyes were locked onto Martin's.

"Thank you, *major*," said Mori.

Stone swallowed hard.

"As I was saying," continued Martin, turning back toward the holographic model of the science station. "The primary assault team will board here, on the starboard aft quarter." Martin manipulated the screen in front of her and hologram zoomed into an interior view of the station. "With the Rangers establishing a perimeter, we'll move to the labs on Level 3. We'll secure the labs and *Yellow Star* will send over a medical team to search for the objective."

Martin turned toward Stone.

"And remember to be on the lookout for those modified soldiers," added Stone. "If we encounter them—"

"We kill them," said Katalya. "We kill all of them."

Chapter 14

Stone sat across from Martin as they waited in the boarding ship as *Yellow Star* neared its jump demarcation point. He watched as she slowly tied her hair into a ponytail. A smile came to his face as he remembered the countless times she had carried out this ritual. He looked down to see her feet tapping up and down.

But they were motionless.

He looked up and their eyes met.

The anticipatory excitement he'd grown accustomed to was replaced with a dark determination that seemed to radiate from deep within her soul.

"Are you okay?" he asked.

"I'm fine…this is what I do." She paused as she pressed the arming pin of her rifle. "All that I do," she said flatly.

'Coming out of the jump,' warned the boarding ship pilot over the intercom. 'As soon we're out of the jump and the fighters are away, we'll get the launch order.'

"Roger," replied Stone as he depressed the 'speak' lever on the intercom next to his position. He glanced toward Mori. Her hair was in its traditional braids but her face paint was new. Mori's face was painted solid black save a yellow stripe across her eyes. Their gaze met and she gave him a nod; her focus was on the coming assault.

'Marshal Stone!' blared over the intercom. "*Yellow Star* reports neutrino spikes and—sir…the skipper needs to talk to you."

Stone unlatched his harness and rushed to the cockpit of the boarding ship. "What is it?" he barked as he stepped inside.

"Sir," replied the pilot, holding a comms receiver.

Stone grabbed the receiver and put it to his face. "What is it, Captain?"

'Marshal…' Stone could hear the anxiety in the captain's voice. "Three Humani frigates are attacking the station! I—what?' asked the captain as he gave out orders with the comms circuit to Stone still open. '…launch all fighters…Sorry, Marshal,' said the captain as he returned his attention to Stone, 'We have picked up boarding parties in route to the station. I'm going to have to divert some fighters to—'

"Just give the order to launch the boarding ships!" interrupted Stone. "We have to get on that station."

'Aye—'

Before the captain could complete his acknowledgement, Stone was on his way back to the troop compartment.

Rushing into the compartment, he sat and latched his harness.

"What is it?" asked Martin.

"The Humani are attacking the station—"

"Is it her?" asked Katalya. "It has to be her," she concluded before Stone could respond.

"Then she'll die today," added Martin.

"I don't know who is in the attack," he replied. "But if she is…" he paused, knowing his next words would be difficult. "…we need to stay focused on the mission. If we get distracted by revenge, millions could suffer for it."

"I won't be distracted," snarled Katalya.

Stone knew what Katalya meant. Leaned toward Mori. "I need you to keep her on task," he said quietly.

'Standby for launch!' echoed through the compartment.

"She'll do her job," replied Mori. "Don't worry about her."

The boarding ship lifted off the deck and the slight floating sensation came to Stone's stomach. "Pilot, pipe us in to the command circuit," ordered Stone into the intercom.

The intercom buzzed and the chatter of the battle poured into the compartment as Stone felt the acceleration of the boarding ship as it leapt from *Yellow Star* into space.

'Alpha Delta, this is Raven-one.' Barked Orion's voice over the circuit as she led *Yellow Star's* fighter squadron. 'Engaging Humani condors near forward quarter of station. Ravens three and four making strafing run on hostile frigate track three.'

249

'Roger, Raven-one,' replied *Yellow Star's* tactical officer. 'Engaging frigate track one with main battery, stand clear of frigate track one.'

'Alpha Bravo, this is Runner-one. All Bravo's away.' Came the report from the boarding ship senior pilot alerting *Yellow Star* all boarding ships were in route.

'Roger, Runner-one—Break Break,' interrupted Raven-one. 'Humani boarding ships have made contact on the aft port quarter and upper midships areas.'

"Son of a bitch," cursed Martin. "They're already onboard."

'Thirty seconds 'til contact,' reported the pilot. 'Midships, starboard side. Orientation horizontal 178 degrees.'

"They're gonna wish they never stepped foot on that fucking station," added Shara.

'Fifteen seconds…'

Stone's stomach tightened as the troop chairs shifted on their axis to align with the station's horizon.

"Remember the mission are the labs!" shouted Stone. "Focus on getting to the labs as fast as we can."

"Ten seconds…brace for impact!'

The sight of Octavius in his arms flashed through Stone's mind. Who would watch over him if he died? Who would raise him? How would they raise—

"Sir!"

Martin's voice brought him back. He looked into her eyes.

"Focus," she mouthed.

"Five seconds..."

With a shake of his head, Stone pushed the intrusive thoughts out of his head; there was no time—

"Three seconds..."

Stone took in a deep breath and gripped the handles of his chair.

"Two...one..."

A metallic *clang* echoed through the interior of the boarding ship as it slammed into the station's hull, jarring everyone in the troop compartment.

'Releasing harnesses!' reported the pilot.

The harness around Stone's chest released and he fell the few centimeters onto the boarding deck.

"Initiating hull breach!"

Stone brought his rifle to the ready as the plasma laser began to bore through the hull.

"Martin, you're point."

Martin nodded, her body coiled at the boarding hatch.

Stone looked toward a panel above the hatch. BREACH LEVEL 75 read the panel, indicating the breaching hole was 75% complete. "Standby!" he ordered as he watched the panel.

85...91...97...BREACH 100.

Stone slammed his hand against the yellow and red ACCESS BREACH button. "Go!"

Martin leapt through the hole as smoke from the laser boring through the station's hull rolled into the compartment.

As Shara moved past, Stone pivoted and stepped through the hole burned into the station's hull. He moved forward quickly as the others took up positions. Scanning the compartment, Stone saw container after container stacked in long lines of shelves.

"Storage compartment; just like the plans said," said Martin.

Stone gave a nod of acknowledgment and motioned for the team to move forward.

Martin stepped forward, moving fast and low between the rows of containers. She reached the end of the row and peered around the corner.

Stone stopped when Martin dropped to one knee and held her hand into the air. Letting her rifle hang from its sling, she drew her sword and glanced back toward Stone. Martin held three fingers in the air then presented her palm to tell the others to stand fast.

"What's she doing?" whispered Mori as she knelt by Stone.

"She's gonna—"

"We don't have time for this," grumbled Mori as she stood and tossed a grenade toward the opening. "Frag out!"

The grenade bounced off the bulkhead and rolled out of sight.

Martin curled away from the edge of the row as the blast sent a wave of pressure through the compartment.

Stone turned toward Mori. 'Why would she do that?' he thought but she was already moving forward before he could ask. He rose to his feet and rushed after her.

Martin rose and pivoted toward the direction of the blast just as Stone and Mori reached her.

"What the fuck was that?" cursed Martin, turning back toward them.

Stone glanced into the small office. The remains of three guards were scattered around the room.

"We don't have time for you to count fucking coup?"

"I don't even know what that means," replied Martin. "But you just let everyone know where we're going."

"They already know we're here," replied Mori. "The whole fucking galaxy is attacking this station right now." She glared at Martin. "And you want to take the time to make it personal."

"Wh—" Martin snapped her head toward Stone. "Sir?"

"We're supposed to moving fast and quiet," replied Stone. "And we're doing neither." He turned toward Mori. "Martin is point. We follow her lead."

"Not if she's going to stop and dance with every fucking—"

"You need to follow fucking orders, bitch," interrupted Martin.

"I don't follow your orders, Hanmani," replied Mori with a smile. "Or yours either if I think it's wrong," she said, turning toward Stone. "You three can waltz your way to the lab if you want, but I'm going to get their fast."

Stone's skin grew hot. "You will follow my orders."

"What I will do is take my team and get there before you, Marshal."

Stone felt his fist tighten. "What is wrong with—"

"Fuck her," said Martin. "Let her go...we don't have time for this. Besides, maybe these assholes acting like fucking battering rams will draw some resistance away from us."

Stone stared into Mori's eyes. That brilliant green that had drawn him in so many times now radiated defiance.

Martin was right.

"Go," grunted Stone.

Without a word Mori turned and motioned for Meadow and Katalya to follow her.

"Sir. We need to go."

Martin's voice refocused Stone.

Stone, Martin, and Shara pushed forward making their way toward the laboratory section. Martin suddenly stopped, warning the others with a hand signal. Stone had just brought his rifle to his shoulder when three Humani soldiers rushed into view. Martin leapt forward crashing into two them.

The third spun and leveled his rifle on Martin.

Stone's rifle recoiled as the soldier jerked to the right and fell to the deck, exposing a row of fangs as he let out a growl. Stone swung the barrel of his rifle toward Martin and the others.

Martin thrust her sword into the abdomen of one of the soldiers just as the second sank its teeth into her left thigh. Letting out a groan, Martin rolled to her right and landed a powerful blow to the second soldier's temple.

The soldier recovered quickly, pulling a pistol from his vest and swinging it toward Martin.

But Martin was too fast as the blade of her knife sank into her opponent's temple.

"Emily!" yelled Stone as he saw the first soldier, Martin's sword still protruding from his torso, rise above her with his sword above his head.

Stone's finger tightened on the trigger but he released when Shara stepped toward the soldier and drove his knife into the enemy's rib cage. The soldier's body arched against the force of the blade and Shara pivoted his body and drove the enemy onto the deck.

As the soldier slammed onto the floor, Shara drew his pistol and fired point blank into his opponent's forehead.

"Damn it," cursed Stone as he looked toward Martin. "Are you okay?"

"Fine," grunted Martin as she applied coagulate to leg. "Just let me..." Martin then grabbed a neuro-injector and slammed it into her thigh. She took a deep breath. "Ready to go, Sir."

Stone looked at Martin's leg. The Dog Soldier had taken a mouth-sized chunk out of her leg. The coagulant would slow the bleeding and the pain killers would allow her to keep pulling a trigger but her injury was bad.

"Are you sure?"

Martin smirked. "Really?" She reached down to pull her sword from the dead Humani soldier. "I can—" Martin stumbled and let out a grunt. "Shit." She looked up toward Stone. "I'll be okay."

"Fine. Let's—" Stone saw movement out of the corner of his eye and spun to his right just as two station guards opened fire from behind a large storage container. "Cover!"

Stone dove for cover behind the corner of the passageway as Shara and Martin pressed their bodies against the opposite bulkhead, where a small support frame provided cover as bullets ricocheted through the passageway.

Stone leaned forward and fired a burst toward the guards. As he did, he saw two more join those that had originally opened fire. "There's four!" he shouted.

Shara nodded in acknowledgment.

Stone looked toward Martin and saw her inject another neuro-med. She grimaced as the needle punctured her skin but then dropped the injector, picked up her rifle and fired a burst toward the guards.

Their eyes met. She would slow them down…and she knew it.

"I'll hold them off here," she spoke into her comms circuit. "You two go down a level and bypass them."

"You sure?" asked Shara.

"Yes," grumbled Martin. "Just tell me when you reach the lab and I'll make my way back to the extraction point."

Stone didn't reply.

Martin leaned forward and fired again, pressing her body back against the bulkhead as a hail of return gunfire bounced off the frame she was using for cover.

"Go!" shouted Martin, waving her hand. "When I die, it's not gonna be at the hands of four fucking security guards."

Stone took a deep breath. "Roger."

***

Martin looked down the barrel of her rifle as a guard rose from behind the container to fire. She squeezed the trigger and the guard crumpled to the deck as two more opened fire.

"One down," said Martin to herself as rounds hit the bulkhead in front and above her. "What's your status?" she asked into the comms link.

The sound of gunfire broke through the link as it activated.

'We're stuck one level down and about twenty frames aft,' came Stone's reply. 'Mori, where are you?' he asked.

'We're still pushing toward the labs,' she replied. 'A lot of resistance.'

'We need to hurry,' said Stone. 'The Rangers are being pressed hard by the Elite Guard and Dog Soldiers…we can't let them get there first.'

"Fuck," cursed Martin, letting her head fall against the bulkhead.

She took a deep breath then held her rifle outward from her cover and fired a long burst. The response was immediate as dozen of rounds impacted around her. As the enemy bullets ricocheted around the hall, Martin dropped her rifle and drew her pistol. With her other hand, she grabbed a grenade and tossed it toward the container.

The firing stopped.

She braced for the explosion and leapt forward with a groan of pain as the blast echoed down the passageway.

Through the smoke, two guards rose and took aim.

Martin pushed forward, firing two rounds into the first guard without breaking stride. The second stumbled backwards while firing.

As the bullets whizzed past her, she leapt over the container and landed on her side.

Martin let out a groan but leveled her pistol just as the guard who had fell to the ground raised his rifle.

Her pistol cracked and the guard's head snapped backwards.

"Shit." Pain raced through her leg but she had to press on. "On my way," she grunted into the comms link.

***

The concentrated fire from the rifles of Mori, Katalya, and Sergeant Meadow shredded the two security guards at the entrance to the lab.

"Move up!" shouted Mori as she rushed forward into the room. Once inside, she swept her rifle from right to left.

Empty.

"Is this it?" asked Sergeant Meadow.

"It should be," replied Mori. "Get your gear and find that serum...I'll look for the data banks."

Mori scanned the room for her objective. They didn't have much time.

"Where are—" A sigh of relief escaped her.

There it was.

Against the opposite wall a large bank of data stations hummed.

Mori walked over to the station. "Status on the serum?"

"Got it," responded Meadow as he slid three metal vials into a pouch on his vest.

"Good." Mori pulled a decryption device from her vest and attached it to the data station. She pressed decrypt and download.

DECRYPT FAILED flashed on the screen.

"Shit," cursed Mori as she pressed the decrypt button again.

DECRYPT FAILED.

"Damn it." Mori turned toward Katalya and Meadow. "You two head back. I'll be right behind you."

"Shouldn't we inform Stone we have the serum?" asked Katalya.

Mori glanced toward Meadow and then back to her sister. "No."

"What?"

"Orders from the Shirt-Wearers. No one else is to know."

Mori saw the confusion on her sister's face and walked over to her. "It's okay, c'uwé," she replied, placing her hands on Katalya's cheeks. "Our people will use this to make sure the Humani and the Xen pay for what they have done."

"But—"

Mori tightened her grasp on Katalya's face. "If you trust me, you'll keep quiet. I can explain all of this later."

Katalya nodded in agreement.

"Good. Now get out of here."

As Katalya and Meadow rushed from the lab, Mori turned back toward the data station.

"You're gonna give me that data one way or another," she said as she slammed the butt of her rifle against the panel lock.

Chapter 15

Martin gripped the rail of the ladderway and leapt to the next floor below. She let out at groan as pain tore through her leg. Exhaling heavily, she leveled her rifle to the door in front of her. "Status?"

'We moved down another level and are coming up on the opposite side," replied Stone. 'Command has issued a recall. We're losing the station and the ships are taking a lot of damage. We'll check the two labs in this section then we need to make our way back to the dropship.'

'We entered the first lab. Nothing so far,' answered Mori. 'You just need to check the other one.'

Martin pushed the door open.

She saw movement and swung her rifle toward a row of data stations.

"You!" she shouted as she saw Mori shoving a data card inside her vest.

Mori spun around, her green eyes wide with surprise.

"I thought you hadn't found anything?" asked Martin, still holding her rifle on Mori. "What do you have there?"

Mori slowly turned toward Martin. "It would have to be you." She paused, noticing Martin's wound. "Where's daddy?"

Martin tightened her grip on her rifle. "I'm gonna ask one more time. What are you doing?"

"None of your business," replied Mori as she stepped to her left, exposing the pistol she held in her right hand.

"Akota cooking up something you don't want us dirty Humani to know about?"

"I follow orders...just like you."

"Not you Akota; you assholes do what you want," replied Martin as she positioned her body to react if Mori acted. "So what's in it for you?"

"I'm serving my people. That's all you need to know."

"How 'bout I just tell the Marshal and let him sort it out?"

Martin saw the muscles in Mori's right hand tense as she placed her other trigger finger to her lips. "Shhh."

"You duplicitous bitch, the cat's out of the bag now. How 'bout you give me that data card?"

"How 'bout you come and get it?"

Martin slid her finger into the trigger guard. Her gaze locked onto Mori's. Whether Mori was following orders or not, she was still betraying Stone. Martin took a slow, deep breath.

Their time had come.

Martin saw a flash of black and spun her rifle to her right. She pulled the trigger but her enemy's right boot deflected her rifle while the left crashed into Martin's jaw.

Martin tumbled backwards as the soldier landed next to her.

She looked up to see a female warrior with shoulder-length raven hair. The soldier held a sword in each hand, her brilliant green eyes radiating confidence and rage.

"You," said the green-eyed warrior, Sierra, a smile forming on her already bloodied mouth.

Martin swung her leg toward the warrior's knee but Sierra blocked her attack and drove a sword toward her with a grunt.

Martin rolled to her left and leapt to her feet just in time to block Sierra's right foot.

Grabbing her attacker's leg, Martin crashed her boot into Sierra's torso.

As Sierra stumbled backwards, Martin drew her sword.

Martin's mouth curled into a smile when she saw Mori level her rifle in the background behind Sierra.

"Goodnigh—"

Martin fell to one knee as the crack of Mori's rifle echoed through the room, letting out a groan as pain shot through her already injured thigh.

She looked up toward Sierra as Mori turned and rushed from the room.

Sierra turned back toward Martin, her head tilted in confusion. "That's interesting."

Martin let out a growl. "Fucking traitorous bitch."

"The Akota can wait," said Sierra, extending her swords to her side. "You're the prize."

"Prize?" Martin pushed herself to her feet with a grimace. "Astra Varus missing something that she thinks I have?" As she was challenging Sierra, she glanced toward the passageway where Mori had escaped, her stomach tight with rage.

Sierra's face burned red. "You're gonna wish I'd killed you when the ProConsul gets her hands on you, traitor."

"Astra Varus can go fuck herself."

Sierra rushed forward, swords slashing.

Martin blocked Sierra's right sword and brought her right arm up to block the other blade before shifting her weight and slamming her fist into Sierra's jaw.

As Sierra twisted away from the blow, she slashed downward with the sword in her left hand.

Martin groaned as the blade passed over her forearm, cutting a gash deep into the flesh.

The two warriors faced each other again.

Martin shifted her weight and her face tightened as pain shot through her left leg.

Sierra glanced toward the blood soaking Martin's pants. "Looks like you're figuring out just how trustworthy the Ters are."

"Ah, they're not too bad," quipped Martin, "other than being undisciplined, superstitious savages." She glanced back toward the passageway. "But that bitch..." Her gaze returned to Sierra, Martin pulled a coagulate injector from her vest and slammed into her thigh just above the wound.

Sierra nodded, waiting to allow Martin to slow the bleeding. "Why do all the good opponents come to me injured?" huffed Sierra. "This might have been a challenge."

"I'll try not to bore you."

Sierra's expression tightened. "You ready?"

Martin rushed forward as Sierra leapt into the air.

Martin slashed her sword as Sierra's boot crashed into her head, knocking her to the deck.

Dazed, Martin rose to her feet and looked across to Sierra.

A gash in Sierra's sleeve showed a small band of blood begin to form around the torn fabric.

Sierra lunged toward Martin.

Martin blocked each slash and jab but was forced backwards as Sierra pressed her attack. Martin retreated until her back hit a cabinet and she shifted her weight, sliding under Sierra's arm and pivoting to land a boot to the back of her leg.

Sierra fell to one knee but spun around to block Martin's sword as she drove it downward. Pushing forward, Martin drove Sierra's right arm backwards over the cabinet, forcing her to drop her sword. She stepped back and cocked her sword over her head but as she slashed downward, pain exploded in her leg as Sierra landed a blow to her wound and pushed upward, slashing at Martin as she curled away from the blade.

Martin's body spasmed as she let out a groan and dropped her sword. Glancing downward, she saw the flesh on her right side opened up.

With a grunt she rose to her feet just as Sierra swung at her. Stepping inside the arc of Sierra's blade, Martin grabbed her enemy's arm and landed a blow to Sierra's jaw while sweeping her leg.

Martin twisted Sierra's body as they fell so they hit the ground with Martin on top of her and her arm locked around her neck. Locking her legs around Sierra's waist, Martin struggled against the pain as she tightened her grip.

Martin felt Sierra's muscles tighten and she tried to squeeze tighter as Sierra pushed herself onto her hands and knees. Sierra's hand gripped hers and began to pull. Feeling her hold begin to slip, she released her right hand and quickly pulled a knife from belt and drove into Sierra's back.

Sierra let out a growl and pushed herself to her feet as Martin pulled the blade from Sierra's back and drove it toward her chest.

As Martin drove the blade downward, Sierra grabbed her arm.

Martin tightened her body as Sierra leaned forward and sent Martin flying over her shoulder.

She hit the ground with a thud and slowly pushed herself to her knees.

Martin drew her pistol and fired but was too late as a kick from Sierra directed the barrel away. Sierra followed with a blow to Martin's temple. Recovering, Martin blocked a knee from Sierra and dove between her opponents legs. Pushing upward, she took Sierra off her feet but stumbled as pain from her side and leg tore through her body. Both fell forward, Martin twisting her body to drive her shoulder into Sierra's chest as they hit the ground.

Rising up, Martin landed two quick blows to Sierra's ribs before her opponent swung her left leg upward and around her neck. Martin tensed her muscles to resist but the pain and Sierra's strength were too much for her and she fell backwards.

Sierra locked Martin's right arm between her legs. Martin grunted against the pain as Sierra increased the pressure and ligaments began to strain. A loud *snap* was drown out by Martin's groan as tendons and ligaments tore and snapped.

Martin used the release of the pressure on her arm to roll forward and slam her left fist into Sierra's forehead. Sierra's head bounced off the deck but she recovered and blocked Martin's next strike.

A boot to her jaw sent Martin backwards. She rose to her feet, dazed.

Panting from exertion and pain, she looked toward Sierra as her opponent pulled a knife from her vest.

At that moment, Martin realized four of Sierra's troops had entered the room and were watching.

She wasn't getting away.

Martin thought back to the last time she had fought someone better than her. The Phelian on that muddy, cold planet so long ago. The Phel warrior was confident too.—and aggressive. Martin raised her uninjured arm toward her opponent. "Come on," she said, motioning Sierra onward.

Sierra rushed forward.

Martin blocked the blade in Sierra's right hand but her body curled in agony as Sierra's left hand landed on her injured side. Before Martin could react, Sierra cupped the back of her head and pulled down hard as she brought her knee up, crashing into Martin's face.

Martin staggered backwards and fell to one knee, her vision blurred. She looked up, tasting blood from her broken nose as it poured down her face. "Come on!" she yelled, spitting blood.

"You're tough enough," replied Sierra. "Too bad you weren't good enough."

Sierra picked up one of her swords and walked up to Martin. "I need you alive...but I guess you still won't give up as long as you are conscious, so I'm gonna have to—"

Martin leapt upward, in one motion driving the knife she had hidden in her right hand into the inside of Sierra's right thigh and snatching the sword from her hand. Martin torqued her body and snapped her waist, letting out a scream of pain and anger as she slashed downward across Sierra's body.

Sierra turned away but the blade still found flesh, slicing open her right arm to the bone.

The sound of movement drew Martin's attention.

Sierra's troops had their rifles leveled on her.

"No!" shouted Sierra as she rose to her feet. "She will be taken alive...and by me!"

Sierra looked down at the knife still protruding from her thigh then up at Martin. "I really wish I could just rip you apart."

"You're gonna have to if you want to take me," grunted Martin.

"You're right," replied Sierra, as she drew her pistol and fired a round into Martin's right leg.

Martin fell to the ground, dropping the sword.

Letting out a heavy breath and a grunt, she grabbed the sword and rose up to her knees.

"You're a fucking warhorse," said Sierra. "I'll give you that."

Another round tore into Martin's shoulder, toppling her.

As she looked up toward the overhead, Martin saw Sierra come into view standing over her.

Sierra knelt over Martin, pulling the sword from her hand. Martin saw blood soaking Sierra's arm.

"It's been fun," said Sierra as she grabbed Martin's jaw and squeezed slightly. "But not as much fun as you're going to have with the ProConsul."

"Just one request," coughed Martin through her blood filled mouth.

Sierra leaned in close. "What is it?"

"Kill that Ter bitch."

Sierra smiled and rose to her feet. "Don't worry," she replied. "I'm going to kill them all," she added before turning to her men. "Bag her up."

***

Stone paced back and forth as he waited for Mori and Martin.

"Martin, come in," spoke Shara into his comms circuit.

No reply.

"The colonel was right behind us, added Sergeant Meadow."

"Then where are they?" Stone felt tense; something was wrong.

'Alpha Delta, this is Alpha Bravo,' all dropships away except command unit. 'Charlie Uniform, mark status?'

Stone grumbled as he activated his comms circuit. "Five mikes."

'Marshal,' replied *Yellow Star's* commanding officer breaking comms doctrine, 'This is Eagleheart. I can give you two.'

Stone let out a frustrated grunt. "Where the fuck are—" Stone paused as Shara and the others raised their rifles toward the sound of footsteps rushing down the passageway.

Stone held his breath as the footsteps grew louder.

Brilliant green eyes met his.

"Sister!" shouted Katalya as she rushed to embrace Mori.

Mori looked over her sister's shoulder at Stone but turned away.

"Did you see Martin?" he asked.

Mori stepped away from her sister but didn't' reply.

'Marshal,' cracked Eagleheart's voice over the circuit. 'You have to leave now.'

"I just need—"

"She's gone," interrupted Mori.

Stone's heart stopped.

"What?"

"I had to come back through the upper level. That's where I saw her."

"No," he replied.

"I saw her."

Stone gripped his rifle tightly "Where was she?"

"There's Elite Guard and those fucking Dog Soldiers everywhere," said Mori. "I barely made it back."

"We can't leave her. I can't—"

Mori placed her hand firmly against Stone's cheek. "She'd dead. There's nothing to go back for."

Stone brushed Mori's hand away. "I left her for dead once. I won't do it again."

He stepped toward the passageway but felt resistance as Mori grabbed his sleeve.

"You can't go back, Magakisca," she said softly.

'Charlie Uniform, this is Dropship 1A Pilot. I've been ordered to leave.'

Stone looked toward Mori, then Shara. "Leave."

"We're not leaving you, sir," replied Shara.

"And I'm not leaving her."

Mori shoved Stone. "She's fucking dead! That doesn't mean we all have to die."

Stone turned again toward the passageway but was blocked by Sergeant Meadow.

"Move sergeant," warned Stone.

Meadow glanced toward Mori, then back to Stone. "Uncle, I—"

Stone stepped into Meadow, locking his leg behind the Akota's and driving him to the ground.

Stone's gaze snapped back toward Mori. "I'm not—" A sharp pain in his shoulder caused Stone to turn around.

"Sorry, sir," replied Shara, holding three neuro empty neuro-injectors. "I want to go after her too but you're too important."

"No. Don't..." Stone's vision blurred and he collapsed into Shara's arms. "No. No," he stammered as he fought the effects of the drugs. "I...I won't...not again..." His head grew heavier and his consciousness faded.

***

"Let's get him on the ship and out of here," ordered Mori.

As the others began to climb up the access ladder, Mori turned toward Shara, who was carrying Stone. "Thank you, sergeant."

"Don't fucking thank me," grumbled Shara. "We can't go back for her, no matter how much any of us want to. We would all end up dead." Shara paused. "But you don't have to look so fucking happy about it."

***

Martin let out a moan as two Dog Soldiers slammed her onto the medical table onboard the Humani frigate. She closed her eyes as spasms of pain rolled over her body.

After a heavy breath, she opened her eyes to see Sierra standing over her.

Sierra's wounded arm was wrapped in a compression bandage, her sleeve soaked in blood.

"Just stopped the bleeding," ordered Sierra. "Let her bathe in the pain."

A scream escaped Martin's lungs as Sierra plunged her finger into the mangled flesh of her left thigh. "Fucking bitch," she cursed.

"Looks like one of mine got a taste," said Sierra as she held her blood soaked finger to her face. After examining it, Sierra slid her finger into her mouth, sucking it clean of Martin's blood. Licking a smudge of blood from her lips, she looked down at Martin. "Tastes like defeat."

"You'd better hope Astra Varus kills me, bitch," grunted Martin. "If she doesn't I'm gonna hunt you down and gut you."

"You don't need to talk dirty to me," replied Sierra. "You're the ProConsul's toy now."

"Well I guess she needs something to play with since she doesn't have her son anymore."

Martin's head snapped to her left as Sierra landed a powerful blow to her jaw. She struggled to take in air as Sierra grabbed her throat and began to squeeze.

"Was it something I said?" coughed Martin.

Sierra's eyes burned with anger. "I am going to enjoy watching you skinned alive."

Martin attempted to speak again but couldn't bring in enough air. Her vision clouded and she lost consciousness.

***

"I thought she'd never shut up," said Sierra as she released her grip on Martin's throat. She walked to the comms station and activated the video link to the bridge.

"What are your orders, Commander Skye?" asked the ship's captain.

"Send a spin message to the ProConsul. Tell her we have Martin and will meet her on Dolus."

Chapter 16

Stone jerked awake.

His thoughts flashed to his last moments of consciousness. "Emily."

"I'm sorry."

Stone looked up to see Mori sitting next to him on his bed. "Why did you stop me?" Still groggy, he swung his leg onto the floor and balanced himself against the wall. "I need my weapons."

"She's gone, Magakisca," said Mori as she stood next to Stone. "There's nothing—"

Stone glared at Mori. "I'm going back."

"We're already out of the system. The Humani have the station." She took his hand. "It's over. She's gone."

Stone jerked his hand away. "I can't leave her there," he said as he sat on the edge of the bed.

"I know she was important to you and was a good soldier," replied Mori, "but we have all lost men and had to move—"

"She's not just another fucking soldier," cursed Stone. "She is…was…"

He felt Mori's hand on his shoulder.

"I didn't' mean to—"

"Just leave me alone," he interrupted.

"Maga—"

"Please, Ino'ka," he said softly.

"We will talk later," she replied.

Stone remained silent, his head in his hands, as Mori left the room.

**

Mori stepped outside of Stone's quarters and let her body fall against the bulkhead. Her stomach churned as the vision of Martin in the sights of her rifle flashed in her mind. She had done some horrible things in her life but this was the worst and she doubted she would ever feel right about it.

But she couldn't undo it.

And she had done it for her people, the Akota. Not the Hanmani, not the lost souls in the Dark Zone, not even for the Terillian Confederation—she had to keep the knowledge of the virus and the vaccine secret. It was what the Shirt-Wearers had ordered.

She had taken dozens of lives for her people with little outcome and Martin was just one person. She was one person that could have ruined everything for her people—for her. "It was worth it," she said, trying to convince herself.

Even if she couldn't convince herself, it was her burden to carry for her people.

Mori pushed herself from against the bulkhead and made her way down the passageway to her quarters. With her and

Stone fighting more than not, and knowing the potential for conflict due to her orders from the Shirt-Wearers, she had asked to be assigned a separate stateroom as a precaution. As she walked, her mind shifted from her guilt to her concern about what this would do to Stone. Even after she was gone, Martin was still driving a wedge between them.

Lost in her thoughts, she didn't notice Katalya standing at the access to her stateroom until her sister called out.

"Ino'ka."

Mori stopped and smiled. "How are you c'uwe?"

"We need to talk," replied Katalya.

"Of course," replied Mori as she opened the door to her stateroom.

Katalya stepped inside and Mori followed. Once the door shut, Katalya spoke.

"I need to understand what happened," she said. "And please do not lie to me."

"C'uwe," said Mori. "I wouldn't lie to—"

"Just tell me what is going on. I listened to you and went along on the station because there was no time but we are back and I need to understand why we are betraying Magakisca."

"We're not betraying him."

"How are we not? You have the data for the antivirus don't you?"

"Yes."

"And Magakisca doesn't know?"

"No. He doesn't."

"Then how are you not betraying him? He and his men won't be protected from the virus?"

"They will. The Shirt-Wearers have assured it. In a few weeks, a standard update to deployment vaccinations will go out. The antivirus will be included but listed as a vaccine for an insect-vector fever. They will be protected."

"But why lie?"

"It is what the Shirt-Wearers want. And they have their reasons."

"And those are?"

Mori took a deep breath.

"Or are you going to lie to me?" asked Katalya.

"No," she huffed. If she could trust anyone, it was her sister. "The Shirt-Wearers feel that if the Humani see the virus spreading in the Dark Zone, they will assume it has affected us as well and attack with a force that is unprepared for the combined Terillian Confederation unaffected by the disease."

Katalya stepped away from her sister. "So you're going to let…" She shook her head. "Let them die?. Millions of them?"

"It is a hard decision and one the Shirt-Wearers did not make lightly. If—"

"No," interrupted Katalya, shaking her head in disbelief. "You can't."

"We have to."

"No. Don't forget I have spent my entire life in the Dark Zone. Those are people you are talking about. People like me."

"But they're not Akota," replied Mori flatly. "That is where my loyalties must lie."

"They—we—are all Akota, or have you forgotten?"

"But our civilization must survive for us to have anything for the survivors in the Dark Zone to look to for guidance once the Humani and Xen are defeated."

"That's why you don't want Stone to know...he'd make you give the antivirus to the Dark Zone worlds."

"And then we would have to fight even more followers of the Word, more warlords, more people like the Association."

"So you'll just kill them off instead?"

"So that our culture can survive...yes," she replied, trying to convince herself.

"What about my people...or have you forgotten I'm not all Akota anymore. Is the wolf-clan also expendable to protect your culture?"

281

"No…we can make sure—"

"So you decide what cultures get to live and which get to—" Katalya paused. "They're going to make you a Shirt-Wearer for this."

"I don't know what the future holds for—"

"Cut the bullshit, Ino'ka. Or do you prefer colonel or Ki'etsenko since titles seem to be what's important to you?"

"That's not fair," snapped Mori. "I am doing this for my people."

"And Stone would care about all people."

"Which will not help us win the war or take back our lost colonies from the previous war."

"Saving the Akota culture through conquest." Katalya laughed, "So the Akota and the Xen are not so unlike after all."

"Not conquest, sister," replied Mori. "We are taking back what the Xen and the Humani took from us generations ago. These planets have wilted and decayed…you should know better than anyone—"

"Don't you dare tell me what I should know. You haven't lost…you didn't see what our mother had to…how she…" Katalya stopped as tears rolled down her checks. "Just don't."

"And I spent my entire life looking for you. All of those shithole planets. Places where—"

"Places where our mother was violated and then killed like an animal. Where I was bought and sold and…" She paused. "But it was also the place where I fell in love and raised a family—"

"A family that the Humani ripped apart."

"You don't have to tell me," growled Katalya. "And don't hide your ambition and xenophobia behind patriotism or the Shirt-Wearers' scheming."

"You don't understand—"

"I never would have thought I would trust a fucking Humani officer over my sister," interrupted Katalya, "but you're making it easy."

Mori's jaw tightened. "It's not about choosing me or him and…" She paused, her skin growing hot. "Are you going to betray your people?"

"What people?" shouted Katalya, her canines showing. "Akota? Terillian? Wolf-Clan? I'm sick of it all. All this fighting and death over the tiny things that make us different…like you and—" Katalya paused again, stepped away from Mori. "Did you kill Martin?"

"No," huffed Mori.

"Did you even see her?"

"I did. She—"

"Never mind. I don't want to know. "

"Are you going to tell to Stone?"

"What? That you probably left Martin to die, or worse, or that you are going to let millions, maybe billions, be killed in hopes of gaining advantage against the Xen when they attack."

Mori stared into Katlaya's green eyes. "Either."

"No."

A sigh of relief escaped Mori's lips.

"Not because I think you're right," continued Katalya, "but because I hope in time you will realize how wrong you are and tell him yourself."

Katalya walked past her Mori to the door.

"And what if I don't?" asked Mori as the door slid open.

Katalya stopped and turned toward Mori. "Then I guess I have no family left at all," sighed Katalya. "And I hope you get everything you deserve for service to *your* people."

***

Martin's body ached as she hung naked from the cold metal walls of a cell on Dolus.

The door opened and the green-eyed bitch that had brought her to this hell walked in.

"The great Emily Martin…Elite Guard, Red Wolf, Paladin…." Sierra laughed. "Traitor to her people."

"Have you killed that bitch for me yet, doggy?"

Sierra laughed again. "Don't worry, I'll taste her blood soon."

Sierra stepped forward, closer to Martin.

Martin grunted and struggled to bring in air as Sierra landed a blow to her stomach.

"But I'm going to do it for the ProConsul, not you, traitor."

"A—and where is fucking Astr—"

Another blow to her stomach stopped her mid-sentence.

Regaining her breath Martin looked up as Astra stepped into the room. Followed by a tall medical officer, two Praetorians, and a man dressed in black suit.

"My old friend Emily Martin," said Astra as she stopped a few meters from Martin. "I'm sure this isn't quite the reunion you had hoped for."

"I dunno," replied Martin. "The reunion's not over yet." She glanced toward the two Praetorians. "I didn't think I left any of those pieces of shit left alive...you know, when I took your baby."

Martin let out a groan as Sierra slammed a fist into Martin's kidneys.

"That's okay, Commander Skye," said Astra, raising her hand to Sierra.

"Skye?" Martin laughed.

"What of it?" asked Sierra.

"I just really fucking hate that name," replied Martin.

"Well," continued Astra as she stepped close to Martin. "I bet you would really like to get your hands on me, wouldn't you?"

"Hands, sword, knife…I'm not picky."

Astra let out a small laugh that ended abruptly as her face tightened.

"I want to know where my son is and I will only ask you one time."

"I don't know where he is and he's not your son anymore, bitch," spat Martin, her sarcasm succumbing to her hatred.

Astra stared into Martin's eyes, pain and hatred radiating from her body. "I didn't think you would talk, you're too stupid for that."

"Then let me down and I'll rip your fucking pet apart," replied Martin as she looked toward Sierra.

"I would gladly skin this one for you, ProConsul," said Sierra returning Martin's gaze.

"That won't be necessary, Commander," said Astra. She turned toward Martin. "I have so much planned for you…so much." Astra slowly pulled a small leather-bound ledger from a pocket in her dress. "Do you know how long I have thought about this moment?"

"Probably about the time I killed all of those Praetorians and took Octavius."

Astra shot a piercing gaze toward Martin before returning her attention to the ledger. "Before that," replied Astra. "Even when you were playing the loyal pet, I knew the day would come when you would have to be put down."

"You listening, little doggy?" asked Martin, again looking toward Sierra.

Sierra laughed. "If the ProConsul wants to kill me right now, I'll hand her my blade."

"See," added Astra. "That is loyalty."

"Woof....woof," replied Martin, still looking at Sierra.

Astra waved her hand and the two Praetorians stepped forward, gagging Martin.

"It's okay, we'll take that off so you can scream properly later," said Astra. "But back to what I was saying." Astra opened the ledger. "You know, people have really lost the art of handwriting. I find it much more personal than clicking away on a data screen or dictating words." She ran her hands over the open pages. "That is why when I have something really personal to convey..." She looked up toward Martin. "And trust me, you fucking bitch, this is personal..." Astra took a deep breath. "...I wrote down everything I wanted done to you...I even categorized it."

As Astra spoke, the medical officer stepped forward and began to place marks over Martin's body. Her head was restrained along with all of her limbs but she felt pressure on her torso, then her legs.

Astra turned the book toward Martin. "See…I have broken it down to mental, physical, and…" Astra stopped and looked over the length of Martin's naked body. "…sexual."

"But don't worry," continued Astra. "I'm not going to kill you…not ever. I'm going to keep you here, like a trophy on my wall to come back to and put my hands on from time to time."

Astra continued.

"If you had been a genetic match, I would have just turned you into one of my pets and sent you with my dear Sierra to finish the job…but you are not that lucky."

Martin attempted to mouth a curse through the gag but only mumbled grunts escaped her.

Astra turned the page in her ledger.

"My plan is to first break you down to the point you forget you are a soldier…then I will make you no longer want to be a woman." Astra glanced toward the man in the suit, who smiled toward Martin. "Then you will forget you are even human." She stepped in close again. "Then, when you realize the filthy animal that you are, I'll make you realize you are nothing but an insect."

The doctor stepped away from Martin and nodded to Astra.

"Dr. Gratis has made some marks for me so I can play around with you and not cause you to bleed out." She looked up toward Martin again. Astra's eyes were a mixture of rage and pleasure. "Take the gag off."

The Praetorians removed the gag.

Martin adjusted her jaw. "You better hope I never—"

Martin let out a groan as Astra slid the blade of a knife into her side.

"You won't," said Astra flatly. "All of the marks made by the doctor...so many choices."

"Fuc—"

Martin was cut short again as another blade slid into her thigh.

"So, you see, anytime I particularly miss my son..." She slid another blade into Martin's torso. "Which is constantly," she growled. "I'm going to slide one of these little blades into you."

Astra glanced at the man in the suit.

"This is Mr. Stansfield. His specialty is pain. He will be responsible for all of the other things I have planned for you."

Martin tried to speak but all she could do was pant against the pain.

"These blades aren't the only things that will penetrate you. In fact, every sort of metal, wood, and species will feel the inside of your body." She looked over the man in the suit again. "Maybe Mr. Stansfield will make a few more orifices for that use if the others become too...damaged."

Martin took in a deep breath. "I'll die before I break."

"You weren't listening," replied Astra. "I'm not going to let you die...you will be here, on this wall, in pain...forever."

About the Author

Brian Dorsey is a retired Naval Officer and is currently a Nuclear Test Engineer for a Naval Shipyard. When not spending time with his family, Brian enjoys reading and researching US and Native American history, watching good TV shows or films (anything by Joss Whedon), hunting, teaching the occasional history class, or working on his next writing project.

Current books available in the Gateway Universe

(with more to come!):

Gateway (Gateway Series Book 1)

Cold Planet (A Gateway Universe Story)

Saint (Gateway Series Book 2)

Uprising (Gateway Series Book 3)

Rise of the Wolf: Katalya's Story (A Gateway Universe Novella)

Schism (Gateway Series Book 4)